By the same author

A Killing for Christ
Irrational Ravings
The Gift
Flesh and Blood
Dirty Laundry
The Deadly Piece

The
Invisible
City

The Invisible City

A New York Sketchbook

Pete Hamill

Drawings by Susan Stillman

Random House · New York

All stories in this work have been previously published in the New York *Daily News* or the New York *Post,* and are reprinted here by permission.

Library of Congress Cataloging in Publication Data
Hamill, Pete, 1935–
The invisible city.
1. New York (City)—Fiction. I. Title.
PZ4.H216In [PS3558.A423] 813'.54 80–5276
ISBN 0–394–50377–5

Manufactured in the United States of America
9 8 7 6 5 4 3 2
First Edition

Design by Bernard Klein

This book is for my brother Denis

"From the ruins, lonely and inexplicable as the sphinx,
rose the Empire State Building and, just as it had been a
tradition of mine to climb to the Plaza Roof to take leave of the
beautiful city, extending as far as eyes could reach, so now
I went to the roof of the last and most magnificent of towers.
Then I understood—everything was explained: I had
discovered the crowning error of the city, its Pandora's box.
Full of vaunting pride the New Yorker had climbed here and
seen with dismay what he had never suspected, that the city
was not the endless succession of canyons that he had
supposed but that it had limits—*from the tallest structure*
he saw for the first time that it faded out into the country
on all sides, into an expanse of green and blue that alone
was limitless . . . "

F. Scott Fitzgerald, *My Lost City,* 1932

"People refuse to see me . . . When they approach me they see
only my surroundings, themselves, or figments of their
imagination—indeed, everything and anything except me."

Ralph Ellison, *Invisible Man,* 1952

These stories were written for newspapers but they are not, in the strictest sense, journalism. They are stories and they are short, but they are not properly short stories as we have come to understand that term. The short stories of Anton Chekov, Seán O'Faoláin, Irwin Shaw, V. S. Pritchett, John O'Hara and Sherwood Anderson are the masterpieces of that form. They have the finished perfection of great master drawings.

But if a fine short story is a drawing, these are sketches. They were written quickly, against the pressure of newspaper deadlines, limited by the rigid space of tabloids, narrow in intention and in language. Most often they deal with moments of crisis, with love and the lack of it, with city loneliness, with the tidal pressure of the past. Some of the people in the stories are friends, relatives, acquaintances. Others were strangers when we met, readers of my newspaper column who had written to me or telephoned me at my office, anxious for a listener. From some of them the stories came pouring out, fully formed; with others I had to dig out the details. What color was the dress you wore that night? Did you recognize him first or did he see you? Exactly what did he say? And what did you think? More important, what did you feel?

At best, such a process is an approximation of factual reality; the details have been edited by memory, or the desire to make something more intense than it might have seemed to a stranger at the time. Certainly my sketchbook was not present at many of the events, and even those stories dredged from my own memories of growing up in New York cannot be described as absolutely accurate for the simple reason that I cannot remember the exact details and the precise dialogue. These stories, in short, are reconstructions, and reconstruction is a function of fiction.

The newspaper form also shaped the style of the stories. Tabloid newspapers are not congenial to literary experiment or embellishment; the writer is speaking to a broad coalition of readers, and if he wants to be understood by most of them, he will write as plainly as possible. This is not the worst discipline for a writer —it has not hurt Chekov, Maupassant, Alberto Moravia, Ernest Hemingway and other writers who published their work in newspapers. In a newspaper, language is never allowed to get in the way of a story; occasionally, under deadline pressure, a newspaperman will overwrite, but usually his work is ruled by the theory that less is more.

I started writing these stories in the 1960s. In those years I was covering war, riots, assassinations and demonstrations with an alarming regularity. I was in the crowds when the tear gas landed and with soldiers when machine guns began to chatter from the tree line. But in the swirl of public events, my own writing was being converted into a blunt instrument, wielded too often in anger.

In that era when crowds seemed to have displaced individuals, I knew there were human beings all around me who were living out smaller dramas. While Martin Luther King lay dying on the motel balcony, there was certainly a man in Memphis washing his car in the sun, worried about his wife's adultery. While guns were firing from the rooftops of Newark, a young woman was falling in love with a middle-aged man on the other side of town. I knew that the majority of people I had grown up with in Brooklyn lived their lives without History; they had fought in wars, some of them, or had made brief appearances in courthouses. But essentially they were exiles from History, forever separated from the past, yet often living that past in the present. As New Yorkers, they were frequently prisoners of their nostalgias. They remembered the city when it was a great big wonderful town and they were young in its streets. They didn't like what had happened to their city. Some of them didn't like what had happened to their lives.

So while I was swinging my blunt instrument against the war and Richard Nixon, I started to write smaller stories. This involved some risk; when you try to describe human emotions, you always risk sentimentality, particularly when the subjects are

New Yorkers, the most sentimental of Americans. I also knew that I could never be complete about these brief lives, that the best I could hope for was to make my fragments as true as possible within the limitations of the newspaper form. In addition, since these people had trusted me with their feelings, I would have to be gentle. It would have been an easy matter to make fun of some of them, to destroy them with irony or glib sophistication. But that would have been a form of felonious assault, because none of them had weapons with which they could strike me back. I didn't want to hurt anyone, least of all the people of the city where I was born, grew up, work, and where, with any luck, I will die and be buried. They live in that city, as I do, with a sense of exhaustion, and sometimes fear. They know that there is a city of politics and government, History and the State. But they live in the invisible city of loneliness and loss. I love that city more than any other on the earth.

Pete Hamill
Brooklyn, March 24, 1980

The
Invisible
City

HIRSCH was shivering when he came up from the subway at Forty-second Street into the cold spring rain. It was already a few minutes past nine-thirty but he didn't really care about the office. The office could wait. The secretary and the cutters and the rest of them could wait. The fall line could wait too. Right now he was going to get some coffee. Right now he was going to get warm, on a cold, wet day in another cold spring.

He went into a coffee shop called the Lantern and walked past the counter into the back. The booths were mostly empty, breakfast finished, the waitresses sitting together in a corner booth. One of them came over, and he ordered a toasted bagel and black coffee and looked again at the paper. Children murdered in the Bronx, a man with hostages in Toronto who wanted to visit Idi Amin, bombs going off somewhere. Fighting in Zaire.

Hirsch sighed, folded the paper and shoved it down beside him in the booth. He bit into the bagel and aimlessly stirred the black coffee. When he looked up he saw a woman coming down the aisle past the empty stools, and his heart turned over.

She wasn't very tall but she looked taller than he remembered because of the high heels on her shiny boots. Her dark hair was covered with a cheap plastic hat and her trench coat glistened with the rain. Her oval Italian face was thicker now, even pouchy, and there were dark smudges of age around the eyes. But he saw her the way he had first seen her thirty years before. He saw her beautiful.

"Is that you, Helen?" he said, slowly rising from the booth.

She stared at him, her face blank, the rain dripping off the plastic hat. She blinked and a puzzled smile spread slowly across her face.

"My name *is* Helen, but—"

"It's *me,* Helen, *Hirsch.* From Bensonhurst. From *Eighteenth Avenue,* remember?"

He was all the way out of the booth now, and she leaned close, trying politely to embrace him, the move made clumsy by her handbag and folding umbrella. She smelled of soap and rain.

"Oh, Hirsch . . . "

"What a surprise," he said, feeling raw and fat and clumsy. "Imagine running into you like this. Who would have expected it? Here, let me get that."

He helped her off with the raincoat and took her umbrella, snapped the loop shut and hung them both on the hooks beside the booth. She thanked him and sat down across from him.

"Have some breakfast," he said. "What'll you have, Helen? Want some eggs? What'll it be?"

"Just coffee, Hirsch."

He waved at the waitress and asked her to bring some coffee, and then he looked at Helen. She had a hand up to her face, the thumb tight against the side of her jaw, as if trying to stretch the skin. Her powder was streaked from the rain and the dark hair was scratched with gray.

"It *has* been a long time, Helen."

"I'm surprised you recognized me, Hirsch."

He laughed. "I'd always recognize you."

She chuckled and the waitress arrived with the coffee. She mixed a spoonful of sugar with some cream, stared at the cup and, without looking up, said, "Well, how've you been, Hirsch?"

"Great, just great," he replied. "Well, not so great, if the truth be known."

"I heard you had your own business. I heard you got married and had kids and all."

"I did. I do. I mean, have my own business. But my wife is gone. She took off. It's eight years now."

"You mean she just disappeared?"

"No, not that simple. We got divorced first. Then she took off. With most of my dough too, I might add." He laughed.

"I'm sorry about that," Helen said.

"What's to be sorry? The world is a crazy place. Just look at the paper. Crazy people everywhere. Assorted maniacs." He sipped his coffee. "What about you, Helen?"

"My husband's dead."

"Oh," Hirsch said. "Oh, that's too bad. You had kids, didn't you?"

"They're all grown up," she said. "That's why I went back to work. I work right down here, near the UN."

"You got married while I was in the Army. One of the guys wrote me about it. I was in Yokosuka, going to Korea." His voice was flat now. "I'll never forget it."

"It's a long time ago, Hirsch."

He smiled. "I had a sergeant that used to say, 'Broken hearts make the best soldiers.' Well, he was wrong. I was lousy."

He waved at the waitress again, motioning for a fresh cup of coffee.

"How's your father?" he said.

"He's dead too. For years now, since 1958."

"Oh boy," Hirsch said. "I always ask the wrong thing. I'm sorry." There was an awkward pause. "He should have let us get married, Helen."

"You know how it was then, Hirsch. It was different then."

"You mean if he was alive now he'd let you marry a Jew?"

"I mean if he was alive now I'd tell him it was none of his business."

She reached across the table and touched his hand. And he was flooded with the things he wanted to say: about living alone and the passage of time; about people they had known long ago; about the night he took her to the dance at Prospect Hall and the Irish guys fought the Italians and he had whisked her out the side door and they had walked for hours in the summer night.

He wanted to tell her how he kept going to the old neighborhood for months after he got out of the Army, to buy ice cream sodas at Jahn's on Eighty-sixth Street, hoping he would run into her in the street. And how years later, when he got over it at last, when it had finally passed and she had become a snapshot in some forgotten album, he had that first violent argument with his wife and had gone out to the garage and drove all the way from Oyster Bay back into the city, back to Bensonhurst, back to Eighteenth Avenue, hoping he would find someone who knew where she was.

But Hirsch didn't say anything. He just sat there swallowing hard, groping for words, until she lifted her hand off his and glanced at her watch.

"I've got to go to work," she said.

"Yeah. Well, okay, Helen, sure."

"It's just down the block."

"Yeah, sure."

They rose together, Hirsch reaching clumsily past her for their coats. He held her coat and she shifted gracefully to slide her arms into the sleeves. From the side the waitress placed the check on the table and Hirsch fumbled for his money clip, looking in one pocket and then the other before finding it. He tucked a dollar under his coffee cup, then stood aside to let Helen walk before him through the empty coffee shop to the door. The rain was still pounding down. Hirsch handed the check and a five-dollar bill to the cashier, and his change made a clacking sound as it fell into the round metal tray at the base of the register. Then he pushed open the door to the vestibule and Helen began to open her umbrella for the final dash through the drowned streets.

"Well, it was sure nice to see you, Hirsch," she said.

"Yeah. It was. It was."

"I have to run," she said.

"Okay."

She turned, pushed at the door. And then Hirsch touched her arm.

"Listen, uh, I, uh, *listen*: Would you like to have dinner tonight?"

"Yes."

"And maybe go see a show tomorrow night?"

"Yes, Hirsch." She smiled. "Yes. Yes."

U S U A L L Y in the fall of the year Sullivan loved the smell of burning leaves. But today, sitting in the yard of his house in Lynbrook, he felt a dull unease, a fugitive sense of the end of things and the arrival of a last season. He sat in the folding aluminum chair drinking a whiskey and soda, with the newspapers on the ground beside him. Leaves were scattered across his yard but he had not yet gathered them; the rake leaned against the white fence, a challenge to act. He didn't move.

He heard sounds inside the house. His wife was back from Mass, and he heard a dish clack against a table and imagined her sliding the roast into the oven and checking the ice and the cake and all the other things they would need for the party. It was his birthday and the children and their wives and their children were all coming, but he had no sense of approaching feast or celebration. He could retire now, under the new plan the company had put together; he could pick up the retirement pay and the pension, someone would give him a gold watch at a Chinese restaurant and he could come out here and burn leaves and sit quietly and, in baseball season, watch all the day games. Forty-six years of work were over, if he wanted them to be over.

"Another drink, Michael?" his wife asked, appearing suddenly in the doorway.

"Sure," he said, without looking around: seeing in his mind's eye her worn, handsome face, thinking that the Irishwoman's face improves as it ages, that this surely must have something to do with acceptance. She took his glass but he stared ahead, watching the smoke drift away into the clear sky. He suddenly remembered her when she was sixteen and they lived four blocks away from each other on Fourth Avenue in Brooklyn; she had lustrous brown hair then and a smile that broke hearts, and for some reason he

remembered proposing to her on a bench in Sunset Park and how they had walked home together in the hot night with their lives spread out before them.

That was the year Babe Ruth hit the sixty home runs, and part of him always turned on the TV set hoping to see the Babe's spindly legs and hulking body and the lovely swing and the ball sailing away to the sky. Gene Tunney was the heavyweight champion and Jimmy Walker was the mayor of New York, and he remembered how everyone that year had tried to dress like the mayor, with narrow suits and snap-brim hats, and how they really looked like Legs Diamond.

"They should be here soon," his wife said, handing him the drink.

"Kitty, what was the name of that speakeasy we used to go to on Seventh Avenue?"

She laughed in a surprised, almost girlish way.

"The speakeasy on Seventh Avenue? Oh, Michael, I don't remember . . . "

The telephone rang and she turned and went back into the house. Flanagan's, Sullivan thought: something like that. Irish. Flanagan's or Harrigan's.

He remembered now the trolley car with slats on the floor that rattled across the Brooklyn Bridge, and the way a snowstorm looked as it moved across the harbor, with the Statue of Liberty lost in the gray swirl, and tugs shoving barges up the East River. It had been his own secret journey: made alone in the mornings and the evenings. And he remembered the private sense of the city's emptiness that came late at night down in Wall Street when he worked late, and the lights burning in the old *World* building on Park Row. He remembered going around Broadway with the others after a big fight, and he wondered if anyone remembered how Jimmy McLarnin threw the hook and what had happened to all of the people he had known in those years before the war.

"That was Jimmy," his wife said. "He'll be late."

Jimmy, he thought, was always late. He had named him after Jimmy Walker, and he remembered how the boy looked when he was ten—blond hair and square shoulders—and the day they had followed the moving truck all the way out to Lynbrook in 1946, with Jackie sitting in the back, Kitty between him and Tommy, Jimmy beside him, and how he had known that day that New York was forever behind him.

They had gone to Lynbrook for the children: he remembered the conversations over the kitchen table in the old neighborhood, the careful calculations about the money, the talk about how the kids needed fresh air and good schools. And now Jackie was already working on his second marriage; Jimmy had worked at fifteen jobs in ten years; Tommy was a drunk.

They were his children and he somehow loved them, but he watched the smoke in the backyards and wondered why he remembered everything that happened before the war and nothing much that happened after; he remembered New York and the rest was a blur; he remembered Jimmy Walker but he couldn't remember who was mayor before Wagner.

He heard a car pull into the driveway, making a grating sound on the pebbles, and then a car door slamming.

"It was Rattigan's," he said triumphantly. "It was Patty Rattigan's!"

He turned and his son Jackie was standing there alone, looking puzzled.

"What was Rattigan's?" Jackie asked.

Sullivan looked away, watching the smoke. "Oh, just a place I was trying to remember," he said. "Nothing important."

He stood, his son embraced him briskly and he started into the house to see his grandchildren, thinking of snow falling on the streets of New York and the luster of a girl's brown hair.

ALL that summer, Peggy Murray and Marty Flood went everywhere together. They would arrive at Bay 22 in Coney Island early in the morning, carrying their own blanket and a big brown portable radio and a newspaper. They would lie slightly apart from the rest of us, Marty's chin propped on his knuckles as Peggy smeared his back with suntan oil, the two of them murmuring to each other and staring out at the sea. We could never hear their words; they seemed always apart, locked together in a small cocoon of privacy, watching the waves break like milk on the dirty sand. It was assumed that they would be the first people in our crowd to get married.

"They're a great couple," the girls would say, and we would watch them as they walked down to Mary's Sandwich Shop at noon, holding hands, to stand in line under the August sun; or see them at the bar at Oceantide, sitting on stools, listening to Kitty Kallen sing "Little Things Mean a Lot"; or later, sitting beside each other in a booth in McCabe's or the Caton Inn. Marty was thin, black-haired, with intense dark eyes; Peggy was a freckled brunette with a dazzling smile. She was in her last year of high school; he was a clerk on Wall Street. They were a great couple. All the girls said so.

That fall the young men started to go away to the war. I was in boot camp at Bainbridge in Maryland when I heard that Marty had been drafted. It was going to be fine, one of the girls wrote me. Before he left, she said, they had a big engagement party at the Hibernians' Hall on Prospect Avenue, and everyone was there, and they looked very much in love, and after all, the Army was only for two years, and they could save their money while he was away and then get married when he got back and everything was going to be just fine.

She sent me a photograph of Peggy and Marty at the engagement party. It must have been late in the evening. Marty's tie was open, his black hair was mussed and his eyes had a dull, lifeless shine like the flat glint of nailheads in a leather chair. His left hand was entwined with Peggy's but she was looking away, smiling that dazzling smile, with a drowsy, tousled morning look in her eyes. For the first time she looked older than he did.

That winter Marty was wounded, along with a lot of other young men who ran into the Chinese Army on their way to the Yalu River. One of the girls wrote me that it wasn't too bad; he was in a hospital in Tokyo and was going to be all right. She didn't mention Peggy.

I was home on leave that summer when I saw Peggy again. She was coming out of Loew's Metropolitan on Fulton Street in downtown Brooklyn. She was wearing a flowery yellow dress and holding the arm of a tall brown-haired guy in a Marine Corps uniform. She was startled when I said hello, and she introduced me to Jack Corrigan and waited warily as we exchanged small talk. She looked as if she would shatter if I dared mention Marty. So I said nothing, shook hands and went off to the bookstores on Pearl Street.

That Friday night the Caton Inn was packed. The big song that year was Jo Stafford's "You Belong to Me" and it played over and over on the jukebox. On the television set Joe Miceli was fighting some locked box of a fighter, using the hook to see whether the welds were any good. On the far side of the bar, beside the back door, Peggy was sitting with her marine. I asked my girl where Marty was.

"He's home," she said. "He got home yesterday. He got his discharge and everything."

"Has he been in here?" I asked.

"No, but everybody's waiting."

Marty showed up around twelve. His hair was chopped short and he looked older. He stood alone at the curve of the horseshoe bar near the front door. He had three or four whiskeys without talking to anyone. The place was very noisy but a lot of eyes were watching Marty. I walked down to say hello and ask how he was feeling, and he answered in a distracted way that he was all right.

He stared past me down the crowded bar to where Peggy was sitting with Jack Corrigan. Her back was turned to Marty and she was looking up at the TV set. But Corrigan caught Marty's look and held it. I went back to my girl.

After one more whiskey, Marty pointed at Corrigan and gestured to the front door. He wanted him outside. Corrigan nodded his agreement. They both started taking off their jackets. Corrigan was pushing his way along the side of the bar when Peggy grabbed his arms. "For God's sake, Jack, don't! Don't, Jack! For God's sake." Corrigan shook her off and went out the front door and met Marty on the sidewalk. All the young men pushed forward to the front windows or stepped outside to watch. The women waited behind. Even Peggy.

Corrigan knocked Marty down with his first punch and kept knocking him down. He was too big and too strong and Marty was too full of whiskey and having too much trouble moving on one of his legs. After a while Ray-Ray Tieri, the bouncer, stepped in. "That's enough," he said. Corrigan shrugged; it was all right with him. But Marty pushed Tieri aside and came on again, his face bruised and lumpy. He landed a good hook, but Corrigan hit him twice and knocked him down again. I went over to Marty as he tried to pull himself up.

"That's it, Marty. Forget it."

"Fuck you," he said. "Just . . . fuck you."

He was sliced under both eyes, his teeth were pink from the blood. He tried to get up and then fell back on his side, lying there in the warm night air like a child who was cold and didn't have a blanket. The ritual was finished; the fight was over.

Perhaps this would be a better story if Peggy had left Corrigan to rejoin the wounded young man who had loved her so intensely for one long summer; but it didn't work out that way. A few weeks later Marty left New York for good. Over the years we heard that he was living in California, was married, had a few children and was doing well in the real estate business. Peggy married her marine. They had some kids and settled on Long Island.

Then, not long ago, one of the old neighborhood girls called me up, full of regret and shock, to say that Peggy had died. Cancer.

She was being waked in some place in Garden City. If I wanted to go out there, could she hitch a ride? We drove out that evening after work, talking about death and marriage and all the people we had loved when we were young.

The funeral home was crowded and smelled of flowers; the children were well dressed and tearless, because it had been a long, hard illness and all the tears had been used up long before this night. I saw Corrigan standing against a wall, his face pouchy and florid, his eyes sore. I told him I was sorry. He nodded and shook hands; we didn't really know each other. I found the woman I had come with and told her I would wait for her outside.

I was standing at the door, smoking, when a cab pulled up. A man got out and reached through the window to pay the driver. He was heavyset and balding, dressed in a dark, velvet-collared coat. His shoes gleamed. He turned to go in. It was Marty.

He didn't recognize me and walked inside. I lit another cigarette and sat in the car to keep warm. I read the paper for a while but my mind wouldn't focus. An empty radio cab arrived and double-parked outside the funeral home with the engine running. I got out and leaned against my car in the chill night air, wishing my woman friend would hurry.

The door of the funeral home opened and Marty stepped out, followed by Corrigan. Marty signaled to the cabdriver to wait. They glanced at me, then walked down the block. I could see Corrigan talking, looking down at the smaller man. Marty's hand came up to his own chin, the thumb and forefinger pinching the flesh. He shook his head slowly. Corrigan kept talking and Marty's head lowered as he stared at the sidewalk, listening. His head came up as he asked a question, and I could see that now he was sobbing. Corrigan said something and then leaned forward and put his hands on Marty's shoulders, as if to brace him. It did no good. Marty leaned forward and the larger man wrapped his arms around him, hugging him, trying to still the heaving body. They stood there for a long time, crying for the woman they both had loved.

They walked together to the cab. Corrigan opened the door and in a strained voice said, "Take care, Marty. Thanks for coming." He watched the cab pull away and then hurried back to the funeral home, wiping at his face with a handkerchief. Three blocks to the east, the cab turned left, in the direction of the LIRR station, and disappeared. I wondered what Marty had told the people in the life he had made for himself on the far side of the continent since his last Oceantide summer, Korea and that night in the Caton Inn. I wondered if they understood why he had to go to New York.

My friend came out and we got into my car for the drive back to the city. She fumbled for a cigarette.

"Marty Flood," she said softly. "I couldn't believe it."

I lit her cigarette and started to drive. She took a long drag and said, "It's unbelievable, coming all this way."

"Not really."

"Well," she said, "maybe now he can be happy."

"Yeah," I said, turning onto the expressway. "Maybe he can."

I was in the back room at the Lion's Head one night, waiting for a girl to join me for a drink, when the fat guy came over. He wheezed when he talked and his feet were very small.

"You're the writer, right?" he said.

"Yeah, I write," I said.

"I'd like to buy you a drink."

"I don't drink."

"What?" he said, looking offended. "What kind of a writer can you be if you don't drink?"

"I'm sorry," I said. "I retired with the title."

He leaned on the table, bringing his face closer to mine.

"I think you're a lousy writer," he said.

"I do the best I can."

"A guy at the bar pointed you out to me," he said. "I heard you came in here. So I ast for you."

I flipped through the first edition of the *News* and looked across the restaurant, past the various couples, at the street. It was raining softly and I could see a few rummies drifting around under the leafless trees of Sheridan Square.

"I read about you in the *Voice* this week," he said. "The guy murdered you."

"Why not?" I said, remembering a review of one of my books. "That's his job. He murders writers."

"I mean he destroyed you, pal," he said with a smile.

"Well, he's young. He might not like murder so much once he tries to ride the horse himself."

"But you deserved it," the fat guy said. "You stole my girl-friend from me."

"I *did*?" Now I looked at his hands.

"She told me all about you," he said.

"What's her name?"

He told me her name. I'd never heard of her and I told him so, but he just wheezed and went on talking.

"We were happy," he said. "We were together four years, until she met you in this dump. She told me all about it. How you took her to Studio 54—"

"Hey, I was in Studio 54 once in my life and a guy took me there to show me around. Another reporter."

"Don't lie," he said. "I know about you. You took her to Studio 54 and then to '21' and then to the Metropolitan Museum! You took her up there and showed her all that Egyptian garbage! You talked to her about books and all, and she left me!"

"Hey, sit down, pal," I said. "Let's talk about this. Do you have a picture of your girlfriend?"

He wheezed and moved and sat down facing me and reached into his wallet. He fumbled around and took out a photograph. It showed a dark-haired woman in her thirties, with sad watery eyes and brackets beginning to form on either side of her mouth.

"She looks like a nice woman," I said, "but believe me, I never saw her before in my life."

"That's a lie! She wouldn't lie to me."

"I think she did," I said. "Where is she now?"

"Who knows? I thought she moved in with you."

"Let's give her a call."

His voice softened. "Nah, I can't do that."

"Come on," I said. "I'll get on and then you get on."

"I can't do that," he said. "She'll think I *care* and I told her I *don't* care. I said to her, 'What's a lousy writer? They're a dime a dozen in this town.'"

"Where'd you meet this dame?"

"Roseland," he whispered.

"Well, maybe we should call her up there," I said. "When my date gets here, we'll go up there together and talk it over."

"She wouldn't go there without me!" he said, his voice rising.

I glanced at my watch. My date was an hour late. "She must have gone there alone at least once," I said. "The night you met her."

"That night she was with her *sister*!" he said. "She's a *good woman.* She doesn't fool around and she doesn't go out!"

"Then what made you think she was running around with me?"

"She *told* me so," he said. "The night we had the *fight!*"

"The fight? Did you hit her?"

"Do I look like the type would hit a girl?"

"No," I lied. "What was the fight about?"

His voice softened. "She wanted to get married."

"So why didn't you marry her?" I asked. "What could it hurt? It's wonderful. It's great. Ask anyone out there at the bar. They were all married once."

"I *am* married!" he said.

Lady Day was singing "In My Solitude" on the jukebox and I wished I was listening to her alone.

"I'm starting to get confused," I mumbled.

"And my wife's in *love.*"

"Hey, I hope not with me!"

"No, with *me,* wise guy!"

I waved at the waitress and asked for a cup of black coffee for me and whatever my new friend was having. I folded the paper and sat on it.

"Okay, so why don't you get divorced?" I said, very slowly and reasonably. "And marry the girl from Roseland?"

"It would destroy the kids," he said.

"How old are they?"

"Twenty-seven and twenty-nine," he said.

"Are you waiting for them to die or something?"

"That's not funny."

"Have another drink," I said.

"It's my round," he said.

He sat very quietly for a long moment. "It's not so weird. I knew a guy was in love with a midget once. She was an inch bigger than a midget. She wasn't a dwarf. Just a midget. The guy went nuts for her. I'm not *that* bad."

"No," I said. "You're just middle-level insane."

"Do I look it?" he asked. "Can you tell it on my face? I mean, do people say, 'Hey, this jerk is *nuts,* it *must* be a broad'?"

"Nah, it doesn't show much."

The waitress brought the coffee and a drink. I looked at my watch.

"You always hang out here alone?" he asked.

"No, sometimes I'm writing."

"What happened to your girl?"

"Who knows?" I said.

He drained half his drink and looked at me. "To tell the truth, I never read one of your books."

"Try one," I said. "You might have a good time."

"I bet you never did steal my girl."

"Easy, pal. You're starting to go sane."

I asked the waitress for the check but the fat guy grabbed it. "I butted into this," he said. "It's on me."

"Thanks," I said, and got up to leave.

"Your girl's a no-show?"

"It looks that way."

"So where you going, this time of night?"

"Maybe I'll change my luck," I said. "Maybe I'll fall in love with a midget."

THE old man placed his suitcase beside the door, kissed his daughter on the cheek, squeezed both her hands and eased past her into the apartment. The living room was large and open, and in the gray afternoon light he could see pieces of furniture from both of her marriages, a number of prints and drawings and a wall jammed with the books of a lifetime. He stopped at the round oak table near the window and turned and smiled at her, his face glazed by the Florida sun. It had been a long time since he had been in New York.

"It's very nice," he said.

"I like it," she said. "It's cozy. As the cliché says, They don't make 'em like this anymore."

"Even if they wanted to," her father said, "they couldn't make them this way anymore. They don't have the craftsmen, the plasterers and carpenters—all those old Europeans. They just don't know how to do it anymore."

"I guess not. Can I get you a drink?"

"Sure."

She went to the other end of the living room and mixed a bourbon and soda. He heard ice cubes clunking against glass as he stared out the window. Traffic was heavy on Central Park West. The trees in the park were bursting with spring and he could see children playing around the steel-colored face of the reservoir. On the far side of the park, the buildings of Fifth Avenue rose out of the trees like a distant wall.

"If there's too much soda," she said, "there's plenty of bourbon."

"Thank you," he said, bowing slightly in a formal way. Then he looked back at the park.

"Well, how was the winter?" she said.

"It was fine," he said. "I spent the days reading about how terrible the winter was up here. I wish I could tell you I envied the snow but I can't because I didn't."

He gave her a warm smile and leaned against the window frame.

"I've got theater tickets for tonight," she said. "The new Cy Coleman show. *I Love My Wife*, it's called."

He smiled thinly.

"It's a musical," she said.

"Good. That's good."

He turned away and sipped his drink and stared out at the park in silence.

"What are you thinking about?" she said.

"You're still asking that question," he said. "When you were a little girl, you always asked me that question."

"I did?"

"Yes," he said. "You always wanted to know."

"Well?"

He sat down on a chair beside the table, crossed his legs and looked out at the darkening sky.

"I was thinking about how it was when we all lived over there, across the park, in the house on Seventy-first and Fifth. You and your brother and mother. And me. I remember how we would look out the windows at night, out across the park, wondering what it was like to live on the West Side."

"Well." She laughed. "Now we know."

"Yes. And I was thinking of a yellow sunsuit your mother bought you when you were six or seven, and how beautiful you looked when we walked together down Fifth Avenue. The war was just starting in Europe and the young men all looked dashing in their uniforms. And your brother wanted me to buy him an airplane at FAO Schwarz's, a toy plane with a rubber band in the middle."

"Stop, Dad."

"And I was remembering what it was like in the evenings in the Thirties when we were all together. The Central Park Casino was open then at Sixty-ninth Street, just inside the park. It was the place Jimmy Walker built for his girlfriend. There was something called the Orange Terrace alongside the casino, and they said the trees there were planted by the Prince of Wales. We all stayed up late then. We stayed up late for almost ten years."

"You're going to get upset," she said.

"At the beginning Prohibition was still on. We would bring our own booze, and they sold setups and food, and they would hand out toy hammers, and when someone in our crowd came in, we'd beat the sides of the ice buckets and the empty bottles. Jimmy Walker came in every night—a handsome, dashing man, he was. In the flesh he looked like that actor Redford. And they had a great orchestra. All the songs were by Rodgers and Hart then. Every one of them. Well, Cole Porter, too. I danced all night with your mother. God, she was beautiful."

"It was a long time ago."

"Everything was a long time ago," he said. "I remember the way I would tingle, actually tingle, in the evening in the old house, getting dressed to go out. Just couldn't wait."

"You wore tails," she said. "I remember that. I remember how funny they seemed to me."

"Yes, those tails. Everybody dressed up then. White tie and tails. And that white satin gown your mother had. I would come home from the brokerage house downtown and start getting ready as soon as I arrived. Your mother would be dressed already. I loved that white satin gown. I loved her, too."

He stared for a long moment, not touching the drink. She tapped his shoulder.

"Can I get you a sandwich, Dad?" she said.

"No, I ate on the plane. Thanks, love."

"You really shouldn't talk about the past, you know," she said. "It always gets you upset. It's over, Dad."

"Yes, it was over after a while," he said. "Do you remember the sheep? They had sheep in the meadows of Central Park. There must have been a hundred of them. They had a shepherd who came out with them in the morning, and they would trim the grass, moving all day through the meadows. Then Robert Moses came in. When La Guardia got elected, Moses moved all the sheep out."

"I don't know whether I remember them," she said, "or

whether I just remember you telling me about them."

"I don't remember the year but Moses moved them out. He closed the casino down, too. He said it was just for rich people. He said you couldn't have a place like that in a park during a depression. So he came in one day with bulldozers and they just knocked it down, shoveled it away. He said it was just for rich people and I suppose he was right."

She took his empty glass and splashed a little bourbon on the ice and poured in a lot of soda. She fixed herself a Scotch on the rocks and went back across the room. He seemed small now, and very quiet.

"Why do you think your mother divorced me?"

"Oh, Dad, it was such a long time ago."

"It was never the same after your brother got killed, was it?" he said. "I thought when the big war was over that you would both be safe. And then Korea happened. I never understood that. I just never understood Korea."

The sky was very dark now and the lights of Fifth Avenue had begun to blink on across the park.

"Why don't you take a nap before we go to the theater?" she said quietly. His back was to her. "We still have a few hours."

He clinked the ice against the sides of his glass. "No," he said, "I'd rather sit here awhile and watch the lights come on in the park."

THE woman was about thirty, nicely dressed, with good teeth and curly brown hair, and she was drinking something pink at the bar of the Camperdown Elm on Union Street in Brooklyn. It was after midnight. The door was open and you could hear the rain falling steadily.

"You ever been in love with a mailman?" she asked.

"Gee, not that I know of," I said.

"Don't do it. Mailmen are the worst."

"I guess you better tell me about it," I sighed.

"It started last year," she said. "I was free as a bird. Working in a typography shop near Wall Street reading proofs. I would go to work at one o'clock and get off at eight. That meant I could stay up late and still hold a job. Free as a bird. And then this Fuentes comes around. A mailman."

"What'd he look like?"

"Not too big, maybe five-eight, and he had on this gray uniform and he was pushing this little cart filled with mail. I guess you'd say he looked ordinary, except for this smile. This smile you could see for six blocks."

"Where were you?"

"On the stoop," she said. "A beautiful summer day. And up comes this character with the mail cart. He hands me some letters, says 'How you doin', sweetheart?' and gives me that damn smile. I say to myself, What is this sweetheart bit? And who is this character, anyway? So I give him a big nothing look. He doesn't look like a mailman to me. He looks like a lunatic. You go around New York smiling at people, you could end up in a nuthouse."

"True."

"So he walks off, singing in Spanish, delivering the mail. The next day he gives me the same act and I give him another big nothing look and he just smiles and goes on up the block singing

his Spanish songs. By the third day he's calling me by my first name, which he learns from the mail." She took a long sip from the pink drink, looked out at the rain.

"Anyway, by the following Monday I can't wait for the mail to be delivered. I get up, get dressed and start looking out the window, just to see this maniac with his crazy, beautiful smile. I really think that man had about six extra teeth. I never came on to the guy. I never even gave him a tumble. But to tell the truth, I did start dressing a little better for the morning. Like I was going to a ball."

She finished her drink and tapped the bar for another.

"Then one day he brings me a package with no stamps on it, gives me the smile and walks away singing. I open this package and there's one of those big smile buttons with 'Have a Nice Day' on it. Written at the bottom, in crayon, is 'Fuentes the mailman.' "

"Uh-oh."

"You're darn right, uh-oh. I figured I must have been leading him on, and how do I really know he's not a degenerate or something? Besides, I'm free as a bird at this time. So for three days I don't go down to the stoop. And when I look out through the curtain, I see Fuentes just plodding up the block. He's not smiling anymore. He's just delivering the mail."

"Through snow and hail and—"

"Yeah," she said, taking a substantial belt from the fresh drink. "And I start feeling bad. After all, I tell myself, the only thing he did was give me a smile button. I mean, that doesn't make the guy Charles Manson. So the next Monday I'm down on the stoop again. He comes up the block, hands me the mail, looks kind of glum, and I say, 'Hey, where's that smile?' And he says, 'You're mad at me, ain't you?' And I tell him I'm not mad at anyone."

She drained the pink drink.

"Anyway, one thing leads to another and he offers to buy me a drink, and I explain how I work in the afternoon and he says 'Oh,' like a hurt kid. Just 'Oh.' And this is a guy who's over forty. So I decide what the hell, they owe me some sick days, so why not? I call in sick and that afternoon I meet him for a drink down at Snooky's."

The bartender came over and put a fresh drink in front of her, rapping the wood to indicate it was on the house.

"Well, he starts telling me a lot of Polish jokes and I start telling him the story of my life. He can't believe I've never been married and I ask him whether he's married and he says yes, and he has another drink and he tells me he can't stand his wife. I ask him how come he's still with her if he can't stand her, and he says he doesn't know, and then he tells me three more jokes. All his jokes are old as the hills, but he's having such a good time telling them in this crazy Spanish accent that I have a good time laughing at them, and later he walks me home and says goodnight at the door. And I figure that's that."

"Only it's not that's that."

"Buddy, it's never that's that."

The bartender stepped around the bar and closed the door. Rain splashed against the windows.

"Every day after that, he brings me some new little thing. A flower. A picture of Mickey Mouse. A little scarf. And there's always the jokes, Puerto Rican jokes. Cuban jokes. Dominican jokes. And Polish jokes. Then a movie. Then he starts to hold my hand. Then he kisses me. And before I know it, I am in love with a Puerto Rican mailman who tells Polish jokes and he's in love with me."

"Listen," I said, "go easy on those pink things. After a while they make it hard to stand up."

"That's why I'm drinking them, dummy. Anyway, now he's talking about leaving his wife and getting a place in the neighborhood so he can be near me. He asks me when is my vacation and I tell him, and he tells his wife he's got to go somewhere for the post office, and we go to Miami together for a week. He says he would like to take me to Puerto Rico but he might run into his wife's relatives, who wouldn't understand why he doesn't like her anymore. When I ask him why he doesn't like her, he just says it's because she doesn't laugh at his jokes. Anyway, Miami is beautiful and we go dancing every night in some Cuban joint, and the last night he asks me to marry him."

"He'll get a divorce and then you two will live happily ever after."

"Yeah. And he was serious. And so was I. Well, we come back to New York on a Saturday night, and I tell him okay, if he gets a divorce I'll marry him. He gives me that forty-four–tooth smile and goes off to his house in the Bronx somewhere. He'll have it out with his wife, he says, and will come see me tomorrow.

"The next day he doesn't come around. But I see this young Puerto Rican girl, maybe sixteen, seventeen, watching my house. After a while she goes away. The next day, Monday, there's a new mailman. I ask him, 'Where is Fuentes?' and he doesn't even know him.

"Tuesday, Fuentes is still gone. And on Wednesday I get a letter from him. He can't see me again, he says. It was all a crazy mistake. He's too old to start his life over. His daughter found out about us and she cried and hollered and made him promise never to see me again. He said he asked for a transfer to another post office and then he said he would never bother me again and he was sorry for everything."

"And that was that?"

"That was that."

"That's too bad."

"Never fall in love with a Puerto Rican mailman who tells Polish jokes," she said.

"I'll try not to," I said. "I really will. Would you like some coffee?"

"No," she said in a shaky voice. "But you could drive me home."

D

I R T Y Sam did his drinking alone in the days when I saw him around Rattigan's, a wonderful saloon in my old neighborhood. He would plant his feet at a vacant spot along the bar, order Four Roses and stand straight and rigid, drinking from a shot glass in quick, precise movements. He was in his fifties, his face was raw and veined, framed by a stubble of gray beard, and in all seasons he wore a dirty Army greatcoat that had been dyed black. He spoke when you spoke to him, but he never asked for favors and never told the easy saloon lies that so many pass off as conversation.

Occasionally he would drop a few lines into a roaring conversation, always in an effort to clarify; he would supply the name of the third baseman for the 1945 St. Louis Browns, or state firmly that Harold Arlen, not Cole Porter, had written a certain song. But he would never elaborate, never go on to please, boast or ingratiate. He drank his Four Roses and moved on.

From time to time, I saw him in other places around the neighborhood: staring into the window of Gutter's shoe store on a cold, bright afternoon; waiting patiently in line at Braren's delicatessen to buy a six-pack of Rheingold; sitting alone on a bench beside the walls of Prospect Park when spring had arrived and the days turned mild. I never saw him with a newspaper and never heard him say hello. In our neighborhood it didn't really matter. Dirty Sam—the young guys gave him the name but never said it to his face—was not the only man in Brooklyn who didn't tell you his life history.

One February night, with a cold sleet storm beating through the city, I left Rattigan's an hour before closing and started for home. As I crossed the street, I saw something move in the doorway of Mr. B's candy store. It was Sam. He was squashed against the door, his legs jutting out before him. I bent down, gripped his arms to lift him and realized that his cloudy gray eyes were open.

"You okay, Sam?" I said.

"Yeah. Yeah. Go away," he said, his voice choked and remote. His eyes didn't move.

"Come on. I'll take you home."

"Beat it."

"You'll freeze to death out here, Sam."

"I said beat it, kid."

But he didn't struggle when I lifted him. He lurched, breathed hard, lurched again, then leaned against the door. He wasn't drunk. He just seemed riddled with bitterness and fatigue. I hailed a cab and half-shoved him inside, but when I asked him where he lived, Sam just sat there, locked in iron silence.

"Hey, if this guy's gonna puke," the cabdriver said, "I don't want the fare."

I told the cabby that he was sick, not drunk, and that I would take care of any mess. Sam finally mumbled that I should drop him at Fourth Avenue and Sackett Street, and the driver slid away along the sleet-glossy streets. At Fourth Avenue we got out of the cab. Sam looked at me and started walking away. I asked the cabby to wait. Sam glanced back at me and ducked into the doorway of a tenement.

"Hey," he said, whirling, "I told you to beat it, didn't I?"

"Yeah."

"Well, beat it!"

Sam didn't come to Rattigan's for a couple of weeks after that. One night he opened the door, saw me at the bar, turned around and went somewhere else. A week later the place was packed with people who had come from a christening. When I arrived I saw Sam down at the end of the bar; his eyes were watching me in the mirror. There was a lot of singing. I waited for a while and, after a few beers, went down to talk to him.

"Listen," I said, "for whatever the hell I did to you that night I took you home, I'm sorry."

He whirled, tiny points of green glittering in the gray eyes.

"You don't know, do you, bright boy?" he said. No, I said, I didn't know. "Well, you invaded me, bright boy. You goddamn well invaded me!"

He turned away and so did I. He was right, of course; I had approached him with easy pity and now, in return, he had stuck a knife into my own doughy sentimentality. I did a lot of drinking that night and for a long time I didn't go to Rattigan's. Finally one Saturday afternoon weeks later I dropped in for a beer and was watching the horse race on TV when Georgie Loftus, the bartender, told me that Dirty Sam had died. I was shocked.

"Last night," Georgie said. "Dropped dead right at the bar in Fitzgerald's. They took him out to Kings County. It's sad. I don't think he had any family."

Part of my shock came from feeling cheated. There were things I wanted to say to Sam that I hadn't yet said and things I wanted to find out. I finished my drink and went for a walk. An hour later I was on Sackett Street.

It took awhile to persuade the Puerto Rican super to let me into the apartment; I didn't even know Sam's last name. But the super obviously thought Sam was strange enough to have strange friends, and after a while he let me go up.

Sam lived on the second floor. When the super opened the door, we both stood still for a moment. The tiny flat was like two rooms in a monastery. A single chair was set neatly beside a bare wooden table, upon which sat a clean plate, a knife and a fork. In the refrigerator there were two eggs, one English muffin wrapped in cellophane and a quarter pound of butter. The linoleum on the floor was scrubbed clean. In the other room there was a single piece of furniture, a narrow bed with the sheets pulled tight in hospital corners and a blanket, folded Army style, at the foot.

The walls were painted white. In the corner a door led into a closet. Sam owned no radio or TV, no telephone, no books, no clock.

"Listen, man," the super said nervously, "what exactly you lookin' for?"

"A name, address, anything," I said. "He must have relatives somewhere."

"Lots of people don't have relatives, man."

I opened the closet door and pulled on a light. Sitting on a shelf were three pairs of wool socks, rolled neatly into balls, and there was one denim work shirt on a wire hanger. On the floor was a footlocker, with a pair of polished paratrooper jump boots on top. A small lock was looped through the hasp of the locker. I looked at the super for permission to break it open. He shrugged and took a screwdriver off a tool belt. I jammed it into the hasp and pushed down. I took a breath and opened the lid.

"Carajo," the super said.

Carajo, indeed. Inside the locker were four women's dresses: yellow, bright orange, burgundy and white. They were pure silk, sumptuous to the touch, and they rustled as I handed them one by one to the super. They must have belonged to a small woman, perhaps even a child. The super looked at them, puzzled, and laid them out side by side on the austere bed.

Folded beneath the dresses was a Marine Corps officer's dress uniform. It was neatly pressed, the braid and pipings gorgeous in the yellow light of the closet bulb.

And under the uniform was a packet of letters, tied tightly with kitchen string, and a handful of wedding photographs. In some of the photographs a young Marine officer—handsome and powerfully built, with a dazzling smile—stood beside a pretty Oriental woman. There were snowy mountains in the background but they seemed insignificant beside the beaming, confident face of the young man.

There were separate hand-tinted photographs of the girl. I riffled through the envelopes, looking at the addresses, which read like an itinerary of departure: Seoul, Tokyo, Manila, Guam. The last address was in Honolulu. They were all addressed to the young man; the return address was in Yokosuka, Japan. I looked at the girl's picture again, at the coarse look around her nose and mouth, the sad grace of her posture, and thought I saw something dangerous in her eyes.

The super and I repacked the trunk. We didn't open the letters. I told him to call the police and tell them what we had found. He locked the apartment and we said goodnight.

I took a long shower when I got home, hoping the water would boil away the dirty sense of invasion that was crawling over me. I watched a late movie on television until I fell asleep. In the morning I wrote a letter to the woman whose address was on all those envelopes, telling her that Sam was dead at last. I never got an answer.

E V E R Y year when the weather changed and the days softened into summer, Delaney thought about his father and how it was when both of them were young.

He remembered him, square-shouldered and tall, coming up out of the subway into the warm Brooklyn evenings, greasy from the day at Todd Shipyards. His father would slip him a dime and give him a smile and then vanish up the stairs to the apartment on the third floor. Sometimes Delaney would follow his father and watch him clean off the black impacted grease with sandy pink soap that came out of a can; or he would stand in the hall bedroom and watch his father open the evening's quart of Ruppert's while Delaney's older brothers talked to him about the Dodgers and he laughed at their naïve jokes.

"I used to wish he would laugh at my jokes or take me on his knee or go out and play ball with me," Delaney told me later. "But I was next to last and there were five of us boys, so I guess I got lost in the shuffle. I would say something and then one of my brothers would say something, only louder, and it never got back to me. But I wanted to know him. I wanted to know what he thought of me. I just couldn't figure a way to find out."

Delaney grew up and went off to the Army, and after his discharge drifted around on the Coast. He did two years at UCLA on the GI bill, worked in an advertising agency, got married and then divorced. One summer in Malibu, as he stared out at the ocean he decided to go home. When he came in from Kennedy in the cab, got out in front of the old building on Seventh Avenue and went in and rang the bell, there was no one home. He walked across the street to Rattigan's and waited.

"I waited a couple of hours," Delaney said, "and then I saw him coming up the avenue. That's when I realized he was getting old. He was sort of bent over and he didn't look tall the way he used to, and he seemed to be all wrapped up in his own thoughts. I came out and called his name and he looked up, and for just a minute there he didn't know me. I had to tell him. I had to tell him I was his son."

Delaney asked his father to join him for a drink, but his father said no, he had to go home and wash up and try to make some dinner.

"He told me he was a bachelor for the summer," Delaney said. "My mother and my youngest brother had taken a bungalow out at Keansburg for the summer, and he only went out to see them on the weekend, and sometimes my older brothers came out too. So I told him not to worry, we could go upstairs and he could wash up and we could go out to dinner. He looked at me in a funny kind of a way. In that neighborhood you never went out to dinner. I don't think there were two restaurants in the whole neighborhood, and they were for the guys who worked in the factory."

Delaney sat in the kitchen while his father washed up, using a solvent from a plastic bottle to cut the grease. He found a can of Budweiser in the refrigerator and popped open the top.

"How was it out there?" his father asked, drying his hands on a blue towel.

"California?" Delaney said. "It was okay."

His father opened a beer and poured it into a long-stemmed glass. "You ever run into that Walter O'Malley?"

"No," the son said. "Not in my set, Dad."

"That was a terrible man. What he did to Brooklyn, they will have a special place for him in the hereafter."

"How are the Mets doing?"

"I don't know. I never watch it anymore."

His father sat there, his body slumped, the once-black hair laced with gray. He was very quiet as he sipped from his beer. Wide freckles of age covered the backs of his hands.

Delaney said, "Come on, we'll go somewhere and eat."

"All right." The old man sighed and got up. "But nothing fancy."

They ate in Felix's, an Italian place on Fifth Avenue and Eighteenth Street, and Delaney tried to explain what California was like, how everybody drove a car and there were no people in the streets and what the smog was like in the summertime. His father listened silently, eating ziti and sausages. Outside it started to rain. They went home together and said goodnight, and Delaney lay awake in his old bedroom for a long while, still on Los Angeles time. Twice he went to the kitchen for beer, trying to make himself logy, and passed his father, asleep with his door open. His breathing was shallow and slow.

"The next day was Saturday," Delaney said. "And it was still raining. He called my mother out in Keansburg and told her he wasn't coming out because of the rain, and then he put me on and she said I should take him out somewhere and have a good time. He was working too hard, she said; take him out. So that's what I did. At least, that's what I started to do."

They started hitting the saloons at nine in the morning, the old man drinking Four Roses, Delaney sticking to beer, and after a few hours they were standing at the bar in Otero's, a Puerto Rican place on Smith Street. The rain pounded down. At the end of the bar was a young woman in a green satin dress. She had glossy black hair and golden skin, and she was sitting alone on a stool. Spanish love songs played on the jukebox. The bartender kept the beer and the Four Roses flowing.

"It's hard to explain what happened," Delaney said. "I was there and the beers were coming, and my old man was standing there keeping quiet, and this girl started to come on to me. I don't know what it was. Maybe it was the rain. Anyway, I went to the jukebox and she said something and I said something. And a little while later, the old man was getting into a car from the car service to go home, with this disappointed look on his face, and I was sitting in a booth with the girl."

It was dark when Delaney got home. The door of the apartment was locked. He fumbled, found the key his father had given him and unlocked the door. He groped in the darkness, trying to find the cord for the kitchen light, and his foot hit something soft.

"I got the light on," Delaney said, "and he was lying where he fell. He was warm. Still dressed in the clothes he had on in the morning. It must have happened when he walked in. He must have walked in, locked the door behind him and then *pow,* the stroke. His eyes were open and he was staring at me."

Delaney called the cops and they rushed his father to the Methodist Hospital. The doctors worked on him all that night and into the next day, and his mother and his brothers came in from Keansburg to see him and waited for a long time in the gleaming white corridors. The doctor came out finally and told them that the old man would live.

"There's a chance he might never talk again," the doctor said. "It might have been better if we had gotten to him earlier."

I would see them around the neighborhood after that, the man who was no longer young and his father. The father was in a wheelchair and the son would push him up the hill to Prospect Park, where they would sit in the sunshine and the leafy silence.

"He didn't last too much longer after that," Delaney said. "But the funny thing was we were closer in those last months than we ever were. Just the two of us sitting in the park. But I never did get to talk to him. I waited almost thirty years, and then when I had him, I couldn't get him to talk. I wish I could have talked to him. I really do. I wish he could have talked to me. But there's nothing to be done about it, is there? Forget it. Don't even answer me."

T H E Blue Beetle was a little guy who once boxed feather-weight, and on weekend nights in the gardens of Brooklyn he was one of the bouncers at the Caton Inn. Nobody really knew if he could fight but it didn't matter. His face was seamed and ridged from old wars, he had the sloping shoulders of a puncher and he walked on the balls of his feet. That is, he looked like a fighter and, most of the time, that was enough for the Caton Inn.

Besides, the other bouncer was a good-looking flat-faced light-heavyweight named Ray-Ray Tieri. And Ray-Ray Tieri was one of the greatest street fighters of his time. Ray-Ray could take out a loudmouth with one punch, but the Blue Beetle ardently believed in negotiation. He would ease up to a troublemaker, say a few select words, such as "Calm down or I'll take your head off," then walk away. In all the years I spent at the Caton Inn, he never had to bruise his hands.

One weekend the Blue Beetle didn't show up. He wasn't around the following weekend or the one after that, and it was clear that the Beetle had given up the bouncer job. Ray-Ray didn't know what had happened to him—if he did, he would never say. Ray-Ray never said much more than "Keep the glasses off the jukebox." He was starting to box as a pro then; Whitey Bimstein was training him at Stillman's and Teddy Brenner was using him on underneath cards at Eastern Parkway. Soon Ray-Ray was gone from the Caton Inn too.

One Friday night a year later, I was at the bar watching Ernie Durando box someone on the old black-and-white set when the Blue Beetle came in with some wise guys. They were all wearing wraparound jackets, pegged pants and gingerella hats. One of them was a very bad fellow named Junior, who years later took up extended residence in Atlanta. I nodded at the Beetle.

"Hey, howaya?" he said.

"Pretty good. What're you doing?"

"A little a dis, a little a dat," he said, smiling, and walked down the bar with Junior and the others.

There weren't many women in the place, and Durando lost a decision in a boring fight, and on the jukebox Joni James records were alternating with the McGuire Sisters singing "Teach Me Tonight." So the wise guys decided to move on. But first they started an argument over change. The new bouncer, a pacifist, went out the front door for a breath of air. Junior threw a stool over the bar. One of the other wise guys heaved an ashtray at the bartender. Someone else broke the Schlitz sign. The Blue Beetle leaned against the wall, his hands in his pockets. Having exercised, the wise guys felt better and left. I never saw the Blue Beetle again.

A few years later, a guy I knew bumped into a long red Oldsmobile double-parked in front of a restaurant called the Cube Steak on Ninth Street near Fifth Avenue in Brooklyn. A little man jumped out of the Oldsmobile in a fury.

"Hey, do you know who I am?" the little guy said.

"No, I don't know *who you are!*"

"I'm da Blue Beetle!"

"Oh yeah?" my friend said. "Well, I'm the Green Hornet!"

He dropped the Blue Beetle with a right hand, got into his car and drove away. Ray-Ray was nowhere in sight.

Not long after that, the Blue Beetle disappeared. But so did some of the wise guys. They started arriving in jails called Green Haven and Dannemora and Attica. Word raced around the neighborhood that the Blue Beetle had turned stool pigeon. He had been caught with some dope peddlers from Sackett Street, the story went, and when the cops came with the handcuffs, the Blue Beetle starting singing arias. The boys in the gingerella hats went to jail. The Blue Beetle went on the lam.

Later, when they started piecing the story together, the neighborhood historians talked about the Blue Beetle's travels around America. He worked in a gas station in Minneapolis. He showed up for a while in Denver. He tried Los Angeles but he skipped Vegas. He drifted through the South to places like Pensacola and Tallahassee. Eventually the wise guys got out of jail, older if not much wiser, and went back to selling dope and people.

The Blue Beetle remained in exile. No one knows how he felt, moving through those alien towns; people like the Beetle do not keep diaries or write letters. He just kept moving, doing a little of this and a little of that, separated by his act of betrayal from New York and its lights and its women, from the gardens of Brooklyn, from the piece of sidewalk in front of the Cube Steak, from a hundred joints like the Caton Inn. He was gone fifteen years. It must have been like doing life.

A few years ago, the wise guys suddenly heard from the Blue Beetle. It doesn't matter how he got in touch; the wise guys got the message. His mother was about to die and she had asked to see him one more time. The Beetle told the wise guys he wanted to come home to the old neighborhood, just for a few days. He didn't say where he was.

They talked it over. What the Beetle had done could never be forgiven. But wise guys tremble at the thought of a dying mother. That was different. So they worked a deal: the Blue Beetle could come home for seventy-two hours, no more. He could see his mother, go to the funeral and the rest. But then he had to go. Seventy-two hours. That was all.

So the Beetle came home. He went to see his mother, who hugged him, chastised him, forgave him and promptly died. He arranged for a quick wake and funeral. And in the evening he went out to the places where he had spent so much of his life. The Caton Inn had changed. The McGuire Sisters were gone, along with Tony Bennett and Joni James; it was all rock 'n' roll now. And the kids at the bar were different too. They looked like every other kid in America, all those hippies in dungarees and long hair and bell-bottoms.

But still, it was home. On the second night, in a joint in Flatbush, the Blue Beetle met a girl. She was tall and blond and young. And the Blue Beetle fell for her like a man driving off a cliff. He bought her drinks. He asked her to dance. He tried to tell her stories. The blonde looked at this small beat-up old man and turned away. But the Beetle was persistent. The next day, after his mother was buried, he came back. The blonde was there. She started talking to him, apparently amused. And the Beetle's heart must have begun to pound. All he needed was a few more days.

He stayed very late at the joint in Flatbush and finally took the blonde home. At the door to her apartment, she kissed him coolly on the cheek. The Beetle went home and slept all day. Right past the seventy-second hour. And when he got up, he walked over to a certain social club on Fifth Avenue and asked to see a certain wise guy. A big wise guy. He wanted an extension.

The big wise guy wasn't there but he was expected. About a dozen men were playing cards in the place and they ignored the Beetle. He asked about people they had all known when they were young together, but nobody answered him. He sat down on a folding chair and waited.

Suddenly two men walked in with guns. They shot the Beetle eight times and walked out. His body slid off the chair onto the floor. The cardplayers kept playing cards. No, they told the cops, they hadn't seen anything. They didn't see the men with the guns because it all happened so fast. They didn't even know the Beetle. They didn't know anything else about anything. The body was put into an ambulance and taken to the Kings County morgue. Somebody mopped the floor at the social club and the others sent out for a pizza. Nobody knows what happened to the blonde.

IN those days a wizard lived behind the blue door and we didn't know it. The door was made of painted blue iron and set into the dirty red-brick wall in the alley that ran through the heart of the Ansonia Clock Factory, which everyone in our neighborhood ardently believed was the largest factory in New York. There were loading docks in the cobblestoned alley, vents that emitted steam in the winter and strange drippings that left scabrous piles the color of phlegm on the gray slate of the windowsills. Everything in the alley was dirty, except the blue door.

The factory, which covered an entire city block, was our Baghdad. We became Ali Baba on its rooftops and fought duels, à la Douglas Fairbanks, up and down its stairways and ladders; we knew all its hallways, the assembly lines where the silverware —the treasure of the caliph—was made, the fluorescent lights— magic white tubes—that were shipped all over America. We were the lost patrol of that Baghdad, masters of all its secrets. Except for the secret of the blue door.

The blue door resisted all our efforts to make it yield its mysteries. We piled cherry bombs around its hinges one Fourth of July, but after the huge explosion had rattled windows and brought the watchman running, the hinges held fast. We tried screwdrivers, hammers, hand drills. We chopped at its burly rivets but we couldn't crack it. Once my brother Tommy and I thought we had it going, with holes pierced around the lock with a borrowed drill and gunpowder from souvenir bullets packed into the holes. But we never finished the job because it was V-J Day and the neighborhood suddenly went crazy with victory; by the time we returned, the holes were filled and the door was once again intact.

Then in the winter of 1947 Tommy and I noticed that the blue door had grown worn and dirty, its surface streaked with rust from its bolts, the blue turning gray as the slate. We reasoned that someone would soon come to paint the door, and if he did we could begin to solve its mystery. After we were let out of school for the Christmas holiday, we took turns watching the alley from the stoops and doorways of Twelfth Street, which faced the alley. We waited and froze in the cold. We waited and saw trucks load and unload, men and women go to work, come down for lunch, return to work and then go home. We waited as the watchman made his rounds of the darkened factory. No one touched the blue door.

On the Saturday morning before Christmas, the alley was deserted, the old flat-bar gates pulled loosely across the entrances. I was standing in the vestibule of Donald O'Connor's house, the glass panes frosted from my breath. And then I saw the blue door open.

It opened only a foot but it was the first time we had ever seen it move. From the darkness within, an old man stepped out. He had a heavy gray beard and wore a long dark coat that reached to his shoes, and he held a can of paint. We were right. My heart was pounding as I stepped out of O'Connor's vestibule onto the stoop, afraid of scaring the old man. He was painting very quickly. I hit my hands together as if I'd just come out to play, and went down the steps. The old man continued painting. He didn't seem aware of me.

I crossed the street, stood behind the brick pillar that framed the gate, and watched. The old man's hand moved quickly, applying the paint with great skill, feathering the brush to make the strokes blend, not overloading the brush or wasting an ounce. He was halfway down the door when I stepped into the alley. His head whipped around. He was wearing small round rimless glasses and his eyes were as old as tombs.

"Hey," I said, trying to be casual, "Merry Christmas."

He didn't move. I was about ten feet away from him, and he held the can in one hand and the brush in the other, looking as if he'd been nailed to the street, and I realized that he was frightened.

"What do you want?" he said softly. I inched closer.

"Nothing. Can I help you with the painting?"

"No. I don't need any help." He had an accent that I didn't recognize.

"Come on," I said. "I'll give you a hand."

"Please. Go away."

"I won't tell anyone you're here," I said, coming closer. "I'm not a stool pigeon."

He started to go back inside but I put a hand on the blue door. He was next to me now. He smelled sour. I glanced inside and could see long tables, vials, test tubes.

"Are you a scientist?" I asked.

"In a way."

"Can you make an atomic bomb?"

"That is a sin," he sighed. "They have committed a great sin. Against man, against science."

The tension seemed to run out of him, as if he had suffered a terrible defeat. I asked if I could see his laboratory and he shrugged, stepped inside without a word and let me follow him. The room was like a cave. Every wall was covered with strange pictures—a huge human eye, the sun, tree roots driving below the surface of the earth, intricately carved symbols, a small photograph of two men with fur hats and beards standing beside a giant animal skull. There were detailed drawings of butterflies and oxen, and of a man with a hog's head. One of the tables was covered with black cloth, on which were strewn dozens of stones —orange, red, green, some of them a polished luminous black. There were measuring scales, piles of schoolboy's composition books, a ceramic mortar and pestle and a large brass pot sitting on a small burner. I looked into the pot and saw a simmering metallic fluid, its grainy surface slowly bubbling. It looked like melted gold.

I turned to the old man and realized that the door was closed. I hadn't seen him close it. For the first time I was afraid.

"I'd better go," I said.

"You can stay if you like," he said sadly. "Now that I've been found, it doesn't matter."

There was no icebox, no radiator or space heater, no kerosene stove, no sign of food. I asked him if he lived there and he said yes, and I wondered aloud what he did to eat. I had never seen him in the Greek's or the pizza store or buying groceries at Jack's on the corner.

"I need very little," he said. "You need less as you get old. You'll see."

He put his hands into the pockets of the long coat and stared at the stones on the table.

"Do you make jewels?" I asked. For the first time he smiled.

"Do you have any coins on you?"

I fumbled in my pockets and found a nickel. He held it between thumb and forefinger against one of the muted lights. Then he laid it on the cloth beside the colored stones. He mumbled in a language I had never heard before and have not heard since. He opened a drawer, found a pair of forceps, lifted the nickel and dipped it into the bubbling pot. He held it there for about a minute and then lifted it out. After waving the coin in the air to let it cool, he nodded and handed it to me. It was still a nickel but now it was gold.

"There," he said. "Thank you for wanting to help me with the paint."

He went to the door and opened it a foot.

"I have to sleep now," he said. "Goodbye."

Years later, some Hollywood people came to town to find locations in Brooklyn for a movie I had written. I moved them through all the places of the neighborhood where I had been a boy. They saw the buildings where I grew up, the bars, the school and the factory where my father had worked on an assembly line making fluorescent lights in those years after the war.

And of course we went to the alley that cut through the factory and I started to tell them about the blue door. But immediately I cut it short and talked about other things. I couldn't really tell them about how I ran home that day to show off the golden nickel and to tell my mother the story of the wizard of the alley. She was skeptical and thought I was covering up some petty crime; but she let me keep the nickel. I didn't tell them that. Or how Tommy and I discussed and then rejected the idea of laying the nickel on a trolley track so that it would be smashed flat and we could see if it was gold all the way through. Or how I left the wondrous nickel in a bureau drawer that night and was shocked and wild with grief to find it gone in the morning. I remembered that we found the blue door unlocked that afternoon, the room empty, the wizard gone. But I didn't tell them that, either.

It was all a long time ago, when alchemists lived in the world. While assistants made notes and snapped Polaroids, I walked away from the movie people into the alley and found the door. Its iron surface was corroded with time. It was no longer blue.

CARMEN Diaz came up out of the Lexington Avenue subway at Fourteenth Street into the first brutal Saturday night of the winter, and she suddenly felt old. The wind roared across Union Square, driving discarded newspapers before it, flattening late shoppers against the gray hulk of the S. Klein building. She was thirty-three now, with a twelve-year-old daughter at home, and she was really too old, she thought, to be going to a dance on a shivery Saturday night.

"*Mira,* Carmen!" a voice called, and she turned and saw her friend Nereida angling across the street from the other subway exit, bending into the wind. They embraced, and Nereida put her hand in Carmen's arm, and they walked together to the dance place on Broadway.

"Hey, cheer up," Nereida said; Carmen could see the hooks of her bridgework when she smiled. Nereida was thirty-five but part of her would always be eighteen. "It's *Saturday,* Carmen. We gonna have some fun."

"I don't feel like it," Carmen said. "I'm too old for this."

"Don't be a *boba,*" Nereida said as they stepped into the hallway and joined the crowd at the elevator. "You're never too old."

There were six other couples waiting, and to Carmen they all seemed like children. The boys were wearing their hair shorter now, dressing like Wall Street executives with vests and pleated coats. The girls were all in gowns, green and violet and black, their skin clear and smooth, their teeth very white and hard. One of the girls smiled at Carmen and Nereida, more in amusement than in welcome.

"Let's go to a movie," Carmen whispered as the packed elevator climbed in the direction of the music. She could hear the steady, distant rumble of congas and the stabbing accents of a trumpet section.

"You sure sound silly sometimes," Nereida said. Carmen leaned back against the rear wall of the elevator, her arms folded across her breasts, and chewed the inside of her lip. She unfocused her eyes and stopped looking at the young people; they only made her feel heavy and slow. The door opened into a large lobby engulfed by the steady pulsing music of salsa.

"Beautiful," Nereida said and walked straight up to a man at the door, a fat Cuban with a high forehead and veins bunched up on his brow. She bought two half-price "ladies only" tickets and breezed down the hall to the checkroom. But Carmen walked slowly, for good reason—she didn't want to leave her coat. Her dress was five years old, and in the frantic hour before leaving home, she had struggled to close the zipper. She thought of her daughter watching *The Godfather* in solitude at home, all the doors locked, and wished she had stayed with her. She would rather be watching Marlon Brando tonight.

"Give me that," Nereida said. "How you gonna dance with a coat on?"

"I'll just sit for a while," Carmen said.

But Nereida slipped the coat off her, flung it across the half door of the checkroom on top of her own and picked up two green plastic discs.

"Listen, *chica*," she said sternly. "Before we go inside, we gotta get something straight. You're a great chick. You're just as beautiful now as you was ten years ago. You been divorced a year. And you're never gonna forget that bum until you meet some guy who's better than he was." Nereida pulled her dress down tightly; it fit her like a tattoo. "Now pull in your belly and throw out your boobies and come on."

Carmen followed her into the packed smoky ballroom. The floor bounced and shuddered from the movements of hundreds of dancers. Across the back wall beside the long bar were the single men, more than a hundred of them, all in suits, their eyes glittery, their hair carefully brushed, all very young, and as Nereida held her hand and moved past them, Carmen picked up a confusion of scents, a feeling of humid closeness, the look of dark drowned eyes and an air of expectancy and sex.

"Two brandies with ginger ale on the side," Nereida said with authority. She paid for the drinks and they walked together to a tiny table.

"Okay, they got a look at us," Nereida whispered.

"I got a look at them too," Carmen said. "I don't know, Neri. I don't know."

"Sit up straight so they see your boobies. If you got 'em, flaunt 'em, I always say. Flaunt means like show them off."

Two young men stopped in front of the table and the taller one asked them to dance. Nereida got up immediately and grabbed his arm. The band was playing a merengue. Carmen shrugged and took the other young man's offered hand; it was small and dry, and the young man gave her a damp, silly smile. They danced a polite merengue, the young man holding her close but not talking, and then harder, more driving music began to play. She did a mambo. He danced something less structured, something new to her. Salsa steps, maybe. She looked around but could not see Nereida.

The young man seemed puzzled at her movements, so she danced even harder. Suddenly she didn't care about him. She was back at the Palladium in its last years, when she was young and lithe and quick; when she had steps in her that nobody had ever seen before; when Tito Puente himself once stood behind the timbals and watched her in amazement. To hell with your salsa, boy, she thought. *Mambo!*

The boy's face looked panicky now and the other dancers were clearing some room for them; the band picked up what had happened and were adding choruses, the conga player rolling hard, the timbal player hitting all of the breaks. Then Nereida was there with her young man, and the circle grew wider as the two women danced with greater intricacy and invention, hair flying, milking the pauses, feet stomping, exploding into ferocious steps, the lead trumpet soaring high over the rhythm and the two young men clearly fading. Carmen's face gleamed with triumph.

And then her zipper broke. Her face fell as it spread open, and when she reached behind her she could feel her own bare flesh.

The moment was over. She rushed off the dance floor, hearing something like applause scattered with laughter, holding the two parts of the dress together. Nereida was behind her. Carmen passed the hundreds of male eyes along the rear wall, heard kissing sounds, among others, and went into the ladies' room.

She leaned on the sink, her head down, and started to cry. When she looked up, her mascara had smeared and Nereida was behind her, a safety pin in her mouth, trying to pull together the sides of the dress.

"Forget it, Neri, I want to go home," Carmen said.

"Go home? Are you crazy? Those dumb kids never saw anybody dance like that before." She pinned the dress together. "Wait here, I'll be right back."

She came back with a glass of brandy and a borrowed sweater. "Drink the whole thing," Nereida said, "and then we go outside again."

"No, I don't want to."

"Do what I say," said her friend. "Every man in the room wants to go to bed with you, and the others want to do it to me."

When they went back outside, a new band was on the stand, playing a bolero. A drunken young man talked to a friend in a hazy, belligerent voice and then looked at Carmen and smiled. "Hey, you can really dance, *mami.*"

She tossed her hair the way she did all the time years ago, and walked past him. The men had not grown any older since she left the dance floor. A merengue played as they sat down at a small table. But nobody came by or asked them to dance. The young boys and girls danced busily and Carmen sipped her drink and watched.

Then she noticed a tall gray-haired man with a trim mustache staring at her from a corner near the exit door. He was wearing a dark-blue suit, and she realized that he was one of the musicians from the first band. A trombone player. He nodded and she smiled and turned away.

"I want to dance," she whispered to Nereida. "I really want to dance some more."

"I think you scared these goddamn *machos* away," Nereida said. "Sons of bitches."

"Maybe," she said, and looked around. The gray-haired man was gone. She sipped the brandy. "Maybe I scared them off. Maybe they saw my fat when my dress broke."

When she looked up, the gray-haired man was standing in front of the table. He had shy, tentative eyes and was not as tall as she expected.

"Would you like to dance, young lady?" he asked in Spanish.

She took his hand. "Only if you take me home."

"Of course," he said, and led her to the dance floor, where a bolero was now playing for all the citizens of the country of the young.

MALLOY was in the men's furnishings department at Bloomingdale's looking at a black leather handbag when he looked up and saw his first wife step off the elevator with her new man. She was listening intently to him, and Malloy drifted behind the necktie racks and watched. She laughed out loud at something and he thought, By God, that's the first time I've seen her laugh in more than four years. It was a deep, real laugh and came from whatever the man was saying. She was wearing a camel's-hair coat that made her look younger than he knew she was, and her hair was longer and her brown suede boots turned the college girl's coat into something elegant and special. He suddenly saw her naked on some distant morning, her hair red in the sun: Basel? Majorca? He could not remember anything about her with precision. He saw the man kiss her hair and he began to feel like a voyeur. He put the handbag down and left.

That night he took an airline stewardess to dinner in an expensive Italian restaurant on the East Side. He had met her the month before at Mr. Laffs when he stumbled in to use the phone, and he liked her bright, chatty style. She was from Chicago. Her father was a real estate salesman, and she had done one bored year at college studying business administration before becoming a stewardess.

"What would you like?" he asked. He knew she would order veal Marsala; the airline stewardesses always did.

"Veal Marsala. But no spaghetti, Bob."

The women who didn't know him always called him Bob, as if they could make up with familiarity what he would never reveal to them himself; those who knew him called him Robert.

"How was Chicago?" he asked, taking a long sip on the Dewar's and soda.

"God, I don't know how they do it, my parents. They do the same thing year in and year out. The crèche on the lawn, mistletoe, the tree. The whole bit. They even have Fred Waring records, the Pennsylvanians singing 'Sleighride' . . . unbelievable."

" . . . those sleighbells ringing, they're ding-ding-dinging for you . . . "

"Exactly."

The waiter took the order, and through the oval window Malloy saw a street-corner Santa Claus walking by; this year, it occurred to him, they were mugging Santa Clauses in cities all across America. And he remembered a Lionel train set under a tree, his son's bright face, the packed feeling of a New York snowstorm in the night.

"They want me to come out there. For the holiday," she said.

"Are you going?"

"My brother is coming in from California with his wife and his two kids, and my sister is coming down from Toronto. I don't know . . . What do you think, Bob?"

"Do what you think is right."

"You don't care?"

"Sure I care," he lied. "I just think you should do what you want to do."

The waiter brought the food and she ate with a dainty grace. Looking at her, he realized that she was fifteen years younger than he was, that he first slept with a woman during the week of her first Christmas and that all the women he knew now were either fifteen years younger than Robert Malloy or fifteen years older. He felt himself drift away from her, thinking instead of the Three Kings Night in Mexico when, blindfolded, they had swung the bats at the piñatas and heard the hard candy spatter across terracotta floors. He wiped his mouth and stood up. The stewardess had worry in her eyes. He smiled, excused himself, went into the men's room and picked up the pay phone.

"I saw you at Bloomingdale's today."

"Why, Robert, playing the spy!" she said. "Well, what did you think of him?"

"He looked all right. The nice-guy type."

"After you, they all are."

"I want to sleep with you tonight," he said suddenly. She said nothing. He blundered on: "I just want to hold you. I don't want to make love. I just want to hold you."

"Robert, I . . . " Her tone was a refusal.

"Please. Just this once." He felt himself pleading, but couldn't arrest it. "I need that, just tonight."

"I . . . " He felt her hesitation, hoped he had touched her own need this once. And then the moment was gone. "No, Robert. I've got a date. I'm flattered but I really can't."

He went back to the table and finished his meal. Over the cognac, he asked the stewardess to spend Christmas with him in Puerto Rico, in a little place called Rincón on the far side of the island. She said she would think it over but he didn't really care.

A dull steady rain was falling when Malloy came up from the Jay Street–Borough Hall stop and walked out onto Fulton Street. He hated shopping, hated the requirements of choice, hated the passing of money and credit cards and the dull stare of the clerks. He looked in the window of a bookshop.

Moments later he saw her coming up out of the subway. Something turned over in his stomach and he remembered sitting with her in Loew's Metropolitan, miserable because it was already over, watching *The Caine Mutiny*; and he also remembered a long walk home through the snow. She had gray in her hair now and the face was thicker under the red umbrella, but she still walked in that odd slanting manner he had seen in so many tall, thin girls in the years since. She had a kerchief over her head and was lost in thought the way she had been throughout that old summer. She was coming right at him, moving under the marquee out of the rain.

"Clare," he said quietly.

She turned and looked at him, squinting out of the long, angular face, and for a moment saw nothing. Would she ever recognize me, he wondered, without pegged pants and a tee shirt rolled high over the shoulders? Then her eyes brightened.

"Robert!"

"How are ya?" he said, feeling pleased and somehow boyish.

"My God, Robert Malloy. What are you doing *here*?"

"I'm going to A and S, to pick out some furniture. I just rented an apartment in the Heights."

"Hey, that's great. I heard you were doing really well."

"It's a job, like any job. Where are you going?"

"May's. Clothes for the kids, you know."

"How about a cup of coffee?"

She hesitated for a beat, looking around, as if here on Fulton Street there might be someone who would recognize her.

"Okay."

He took the umbrella in his right hand, with Clare on his left, and they stepped out into the rain, heading for a luncheonette he knew on Livingston Street. He remembered her tense, almost clenched body and was careful not to touch her. She must be thirty-six now, he thought; and I haven't seen her since we were both eighteen. Half a lifetime.

"Where do you live now, Clare?"

"Out near Shore Parkway. We bought a house there, God, ten years ago. I've got four kids now."

"Boys or girls?"

"All girls," she said, smiling shyly. "The youngest is three."

"Hey, that's great."

"What about you?"

"Two boys."

"Your wife must like that—the boys, I mean."

"I'm divorced."

"Oh," she said, looking at him under the umbrella. "I'm sorry to hear that. I really am."

They turned onto Livingston Street in silence, but the luncheonette he remembered was gone, the way Namm's was gone and Loeser's was gone and 1953 was gone. He saw another one a block away and started walking with her more quickly.

The luncheonette smelled of onions and grease and wet wool, and they sat at a table near the window; the plastic top was spattered with crumbs. He ordered two cups of coffee and two English muffins.

"How's Billy?" he asked.

"Billy?" She looked at him carefully and seemed puzzled. "Oh, Billy Colbert. Gee, I don't really know, Robert, I—"

"You didn't marry him?"

"Oh God, no." She laughed. "I haven't seen him since . . . well, since you went away that time."

Something tossed in his stomach again, something made up of a walk in the snow, a conversation on a cold porch, regret, a Greyhound plowing through the night across the country and old jealousy, a sense of fracture and tearing. He had seen her parked in a car with Colbert, heard the long night of explanation and had gone.

"I've got to be off, Robert," she said quietly. "It really has been nice seeing you again. I always knew you'd do well."

"Well," he said, smiling thinly. "Clare, I . . . I'd really like to see you sometime, you know, for a drink or something."

He was sorry as soon as he said it. Her face went flat again and squinted.

"Robert, I'm married . . . "

"I know. I'm sorry."

He shook her thin hand. She smiled, walked to the door and turned out into the crowd. He sat over his coffee for a long while and then he stepped out into the rain, heading for the subway and shuddering in the cold.

W H E N he woke up, Erskine thought he had gone deaf. At some point in the night, all the sounds of the city had stopped. He couldn't hear Big Alice wheezing in her room across the hall. He heard no sirens splitting the air of Eighth Avenue. Most of all, he could hear no children.

Usually the children brought him to life each morning in the furnished room off the avenue on Seventeenth Street. He didn't understand the little ones who shouted to each other in Spanish or made clanging toys of pots and pans. But they always smiled at him when he came out into the hall and went to wash in the bathroom. They were never the same children for more than a month or two, because they always arrived in the wake of some fire in the Bronx or Brooklyn, sent here for a few nights by The Welfare before moving again to some other wild and dangerous corner of the city.

This morning was different. Bright sunlight leaked under the bottom of the dirty bottle-green window shade, so he knew it was day. He wished he knew the time but it had been a long while since he had lived his life by watches or clocks. He lay there very still, enjoying and fearing the emptiness. Something moved between the walls: a scratch, a slither, a hard brown tail slapping against plasterboard. The rats urged him to rise.

He pulled on socks, shoes and trousers, grabbed a towel and razor and went out into the hall. Big Alice was coming out of the bathroom, her round coal-black face scrubbed clean of all marks, including eyebrows.

"Where'd everybody go?" Erskine asked.

"Fawt' of July," Big Alice said, as if that explained everything. She edged past him and wheezed. Her huge bulk was somehow reassuring, and Erskine went into the narrow bathroom, lathered with the hand soap and started pulling the razor across his maple-colored face.

The Fourth of July. He remembered the thick heat of Columbia, South Carolina, when he was a boy: the sounds of insects, the smell of freshly cut grass and the big fish fry with all the war veterans. Great tall black men who had been to places like Italy and France and the Pacific. There were brass bands and tents and endless games in the open fields behind the churches. His mother moved around after the children, keeping them out of trouble with a quick bump of the hip or a tug of the hair. All the while the brass bands played while the kids waited for the night.

Erskine finished shaving, threw tepid water on his face and dried with the towel. At night the fireworks broke up the sky. Rockets headed for the moon. Great careening wheels of light turned and spun against the backdrop of summer stars. There were shocking bursts of red, white and blue, followed by explosions that made the earth tremble. Children squealed and shouted and the women gasped, and the great tall veterans smiled at each other in a cool and knowing way.

That was all so long ago: before the machines came and the farms emptied and the men started moving north, followed by the women and children. It was before Erskine's family took the bus to Washington, and before they packed up again and went on to Brooklyn, where his father was supposed to be living. He had sent them a postcard, saying he would meet them at the Port Authority Bus Terminal. But when they arrived he wasn't there. His father was never there again. His father was gone, along with the fireworks and the sound of insects and the smell of freshly cut grass.

Erskine put on his blue sleeveless shirt, locked the door and went out into the empty streets. A cool summer breeze blew along Eighth Avenue. He walked uptown, ate some eggs in a restaurant on Twenty-second Street, saw that it was a little after eleven and started walking again. He wanted a drink but this was Sunday and the bars were still closed. There were no children anywhere.

Erskine suddenly wanted to see his own kids. It had been months now, maybe longer. He couldn't really remember because in the room on Seventeenth Street one day became another and there was just enough money for the rent and some food and a little wine. He stepped into a pay phone but the coin-return slot was twisted and ripped, as if blown apart. Probably a cherry bomb. Or one of those M-80s. It's the Fourth of July, he thought, and the kids are blowing things up.

Near Madison Square Garden he found a phone that worked. He couldn't remember the number of the apartment on De Kalb Avenue, so he called information. They found the number, but when he dropped the dime again and started to dial, Erskine couldn't complete the call. She was so fierce with him the last time they talked that he had stayed drunk for four days. Fierce about money. Fierce about the way he'd ruined her life. He hung up.

Erskine walked some more, thinking about his two boys and his daughter. The girl would be all right; she was smart and read books. But he worried about the boys. They could get hurt. Run with the wrong crowd. Dope. Some dumb night with a gun. Any kind of thing. Boys could get hurt. Women were really tougher than men. Nobody knew that better than Erskine.

He went into the next undamaged pay phone and dialed quickly. His stomach tightened. His hands were sweating. He could hear the phone ringing—and ringing, and ringing some more—and knew that they were all out somewhere. Gone to some beach. To Coney Island. To hot dogs and buttered corn and orange soda. He hung up, engulfed in solitude.

A Blarney Stone was open now. He went in and had two shots of Canadian Club, feeling the amber warmth knifing into his stomach. He dried his sweating hands on his trousers. The bartender was a frosty white man reading the *Daily News* under the television set. Erskine wanted to talk to someone, so he went to the pay phone and called me at the paper.

I hadn't heard from him in years. He talked about that time in the Navy, in 1953 in Pensacola, when the bus driver wouldn't take us back to Ellyson Field because Erskine was supposed to sit in the back and we had refused to move; the cops came and took us away in our dress whites and drove us to the main gate of the base. He remembered a night in Mobile when we saw Tab Smith play tenor in a joint called the Black Cat Club and ended up the next morning on the second-floor porch of Madame Belle's joint, with the girls making a fuss and feeding us grits.

"Hey, those were good times," Erskine said.

"They sure were," I said. And then for a long hour after I called him back, he told me about some of the bad times. When we finished talking, he had another whiskey and walked back out into the streets. He drifted along until he found himself across the street from the Port Authority Bus Terminal.

A few drowsy hookers tiptoed to their assigned posts on Eighth Avenue. Cops lounged in the shade, thumbs looped into their gun belts. A few people came out of the terminal and piled into waiting cabs. Erskine crossed the street and went into the bus station.

He drifted around, looking at the faces. Then, on the second level, he saw a heavyset black woman and two children, looking lost and baffled. The woman's clothes were wrinkled from a long night's ride. She was talking to the little boy, and the boy bent down and started tying his shoelace. He tied the lace the way Erskine still tied his, and when the boy finished and looked up at his mother, Erskine began to cry.

He turned around quickly so nobody could see him crying, and hurried down the stairs and out of the terminal. He never looked back.

T H E Y bought the brownstone in Brooklyn in the third summer of their marriage. Every day Marsha left their baby with her mother while she and Sam worked on the four-story building, stripping away the scar tissue of the last thirty years of its life.

"I'm gonna get it right back to the nineteenth century," Sam told me. "No TV sets, radios, nothing. I want it the way it was."

With steel wool and wire brushes, they removed layers of scabrous paint from the woodwork on the ground floor. They cleaned out the runners where sliding double doors had once moved easily, and they stripped and restored the doors. The wall in the kitchen had been covered with a skin of cheap plaster, which they chopped away to expose the original brick.

Their bodies ached. Their hair was always matted and powdered with dust. But with each new assault on the twentieth century they grew happier. When I met Sam in the street, he would be almost giddy with pleasure as he described his latest victory over plasterboard, linoleum, cheap paint or fluorescent lights.

They hadn't yet heard the voices.

"I want to have the greatest housewarming in the history of Park Slope," Sam said. "I'd like to have everyone come in horse and carriage. No cars. No taxis."

Sam, a stockbroker, let his beard grow; Marsha stopped wearing makeup. They began to collect old engravings, copies of *Harper's Weekly,* reproductions of cartoons by Thomas Nast. The work went on. And when the ground floor was finished, they moved in. They had found an old fourposter bed which barely fit into the small ground-floor room, but they knew that when they finished the upper stories and could sleep in the giant master bedroom, the bed would seem tiny. The day they moved in, Marsha brought along a delicately wrought wicker bassinet for the baby. They had an elegant candlelight dinner and then went to bed.

That night they heard the voices. One of the voices belonged to a young woman. The words were indistinct but the tone was full of sorrow. The other belonged to a man. It was deeper, the words more clipped.

Marsha woke up first. "Sam," she said. "Wake up, Sam."

He woke up and lay still, feeling strange, as people usually do when they wake up in a new room.

"There's someone in the house," Marsha whispered.

Sam lay very still, listening. He could hear traffic moving outside, a few lone cars heading up the slope to Prospect Park. He waited for the squeak of a floorboard, the sound of an intruder. His body tensed. He did not own a gun. And he was not a fighter. He lay there in the dark.

And then he heard the voices too. Somewhere upstairs.

A man. A young woman.

The woman's voice was a long, low croon. Pleading, as if asking the man to stay. The man's voice was abrupt.

Sam switched on the bed light, his back pebbled with fear. He pulled a bathrobe over his pajamas and went to the kitchen. He found the flashlight under the sink and picked up the heavy leg of a table he had bought at the flea market and had been planning to repair. He told his wife to dress the baby and wait by the door, and then he went up the stairs.

"Who's there?" he said, playing the light over the heaped mounds of broken board, paint cans, tools and clutter. Nobody answered and he heard no sound. He went to the next floor and then to the top floor and saw nothing. A ladder led to the attic.

"I wanted to get out of there," he told me later, "but I knew if I didn't go up there, I'd never be able to sleep. So I went up to the attic and looked around. But it was absolutely empty."

That night they joked over a bottle of wine and talked about the strange sounds the wind makes in old houses, laughed some more and kidded about ghosts, and after a while they fell asleep.

The next night they heard the voices again.

The woman's voice, imploring and sad and young. The man

curt, older, more definite. Sam's heart rapped against his chest. Marsha gripped his hand. They lay there until the voices went away and then they slowly eased into sleep.

For a week they heard nothing. They finished the parlor floor and moved in more furniture on a Saturday morning. That evening they sat sipping wine in the rich shadows cast by the crystal chandelier. The polished parquet floors gleamed and the baby crawled from one end of the room to the other like a puppy, examining the limits of the world. Sam drew the drapes, sealing out the twentieth century.

That night they heard footsteps.

The sharp, heavy heels of a man's boots moved across the ceiling over their bed, followed by the smaller tapping sound of a woman's steps. The footsteps were followed by the voices: the woman's imploring, the man's curtly refusing.

They lay awake until daylight leaked under the shades.

"You've got to come and stay with us," Sam said to me one afternoon. He looked sick and ragged as he told me the story. He said Marsha was breaking out in hives, her energy drained. "You've got to come over."

I went over that night and slept on a couch in the parlor. I heard absolutely nothing except the thin whine of traffic. In the morning Sam and Marsha were very quiet, almost ashamed of themselves.

"Maybe we've just been working too hard on the house," Sam said. "It could be some weird kind of hysteria."

That night they heard a door slam on the parlor floor and the woman's voice weeping hysterically. Sam ran up the stairs. The door was shut tight. Nobody was there and there were no other sounds. He went downstairs slowly, looked at the baby, consoled Marsha and went to bed. When he put out the light, they heard the woman's uncontrollable sobbing again. That night Marsha cried herself to sleep.

Sam still believed in reason. He had a carpenter examine every beam and brick in the house, but the man found nothing. He researched the history of the house, tracing it back to its construction in 1884. He found the names of the six previous owners, but the real estate records were bald, legalistic and oddly mute. Still, he asked me to look up the former owners in the library of the newspaper where I worked. I did but there was nothing under any of the names.

"I hope you don't think I'm nuts," he said somberly. "I just want to check out everything."

For almost a month Sam and Marsha heard nothing. On the night that they finished the top floor, they moved the fourposter into the master bedroom. As they expected, the bed looked tiny. There was a working fireplace against one wall and a view of an old maple tree in the yard. The baby's room was at the other end of the floor, facing the street.

That night they heard music. The long, low trilling of a harp, full of melancholy and departure. There were no voices. Just the sound of the harp. A sound right out of the nineteenth century.

Once more Sam pulled himself out of bed, found the flashlight and climbed the ladder to the attic. The long low-ceilinged space was empty. He stood there under the roof holding the flashlight and heard the harp again. It was very close, each note very clear. He scanned the attic with the light and saw nothing. Nothing at all. But the harp played, calling to him across the years, and he sat down with his back against a beam, staring into the darkness.

A week later I saw Sam in the street. He had shaved his beard and seemed happy. He told me that he had been reassigned to California. Marsha was very happy. It would be great for the baby. He could play a lot of tennis. The house was for sale.

T

H E thing everyone remembered later was that Soldier had beautiful hands. He would come storming into the White Rose on Fourteenth Street, blinded with rage or anger, the Army greatcoat stained and frayed, his thick-lidded ex-fighter's face rheumy with defeat, and yet the hands would perform as if they belonged to somebody else. I suppose that is why the Mex loved him.

It wasn't that the components of those hands had anything going for them. The fingers, the left thumb, the tops of each hand were mashed and crumpled, casualties of too many street fights, too many bad nights in rotten places. There were no knuckles at all on the right hand, just deep dimples where they used to be. But the hands had a kind of elegance in spite of their parts.

Sometimes Soldier looked like some minor British officer, drinking his Fleischmann's and beer as if it were tea in a country parsonage. But the extended pinkie was only a hint; Soldier's hands performed, they did not merely pose.

He would come into the White Rose and take a place at the bar, and when he started to talk, the Mex would slide up beside him and listen. The stories were always the same: about a woman named Lorna, about the time he boxed Young Stribling in Savannah, about the lieutenant he flattened at Fort Dix in 1940 and the guards he flattened later in the stockade and the time the MPs locked him up in Honolulu.

When he was asked about the present, his hands were always flat on the bar or gripping a glass. But when he talked about the past, the hands sculpted violent or gorgeous images. The fights came alive, but so did Lorna, emerging full-blown out of the air as the hands touched her vanished hair or kneaded her long-gone body. "She was a good, sweet girlie-o," Soldier would say. "Good, sweet girlie-o." But he never had to explain; Lorna was there with us in the White Rose. Other nights the hands would describe the hill country in Arkansas, the flight of birds in the morning, the course of a river, all those things that were Soldier's life before he went off to the Army and later landed in New York. Late at night when the TV was off, the Mex would play out his own bad times for Soldier on a mouth organ. But Soldier didn't listen well.

"Don't hear nothin' and you don't get hurt," Soldier would say, and when he got in jams, when the nights would explode into blood and pain, it wasn't because someone had wounded him with a word, but because they didn't understand his loud private shouts. "Johnnie the horse, the moon is out," Soldier would shout. And never explain. Only the Mex seemed to understand and he wasn't telling.

The Mex had come to New York from Amarillo, through Kansas City and the Army, and he was a member of the Church of the Nazarene. He worked for a while at the Waldorf and as a busboy at Manuche's, but that was only to eat; he was into salvation, specifically the salvation of Soldier. "I doan wanna save the world," he said one night. "Just Soldier."

After a while he and Soldier shared a room together, in a cheap hotel near Fourth Avenue. You would see them sometimes in the morning, the little man talking about God and the Second Coming, the older man silent, his hands stuffed into the pockets of the coat. But the day had little to do with Soldier or the Mex. Life on that street began at dusk. We would come out of the Gramercy Gym on Fourteenth Street after a workout, and there in front of the automat across the street would stand Soldier and the Mex. "Johnnie the horse, the moon is out," he would shout at the sky as limousines pulled up in front of Lüchow's and young fighters laughed. One rainy night I saw Zsa Zsa Gabor get out of a car and flee into the restaurant in panic while Soldier was shouting. Johnnie the horse? The *moon*, while it was *raining*?

One night I stopped in the White Rose for a beer. The Mex was alone at the end of the bar, looking sour and forlorn. I asked him where Soldier was. "Gone," the Mex said. Dead? "I doan know. He jus' never came home." He had been gone three months. The Mex had called Bellevue and the police, but wherever he was, Soldier had left no trace.

"I think he jus' wen' home," the Mex said. "Someplace."

We had a few drinks together. The Mex said that he wasn't really worried, that God would take care of Soldier. But he didn't sound convinced. "One of the las' things I asked him was, you know, did he believe in God? He said he didden know, he didden know what a God was. But you know, it was funny, his hands . . . "

The Mex didn't finish. There was a football game on the TV, someone shouted and there was an argument near the front door. Quietly the Mex started to play on the harmonica, as if to soothe the world the way he had so often soothed Soldier. He was playing there alone when I picked up my change to go home. The moon was out, clean and perfect, as if shaped by Soldier's hands.

M

ALLOY waited alone at the bar at Jimmy's on West Fifty-seventh Street, eating too many peanuts and smoking too much, wondering if he would recognize Harrington when he came in the door. He vaguely remembered him in U.S. Navy blues, hat cocked back on his head, gabby and funny. But Malloy started counting after Harrington's phone call, and it was eighteen years since he had seen him, and nobody looked the same after eighteen years of anything. He gazed out at the gloomy street.

"This is the worst day yet," said the bartender. "We might never see the sun again."

"We haven't seen the sun since Nixon got reelected, Dan," Malloy said. "God must be angry with us."

He sipped the beer and looked up and saw a short, stocky man in horn-rimmed glasses taking off his coat and talking to the hatcheck girl. She motioned to the bar and the man looked around, squinting. It was Harrington, all right. Malloy waved and the man came over.

"Hey," Harrington said, shaking hands, "it's been a long time. How are ya, Bobby?"

"Pretty good," Malloy said. "What are you drinking?"

He ordered Scotch and water for Harrington and another beer for himself, and thought, This is stupid, there's nothing to say. But Harrington talked anyway: about how he had seen Malloy's name in some gossip column, and how he wrote for the address and phone number, and how was Malloy doing, anyway? Harrington was "in hotel management," he said, lived outside of Cleveland, had three kids and voted for Nixon. Eighteen years. They ordered another round. The talk was routine, stale. Malloy wished the phone would ring and rescue him.

"Did you ever go back?" Harrington asked after a while.

"Where?"

"You know where," Harrington said. He was staring across the bar at a plump blonde who was talking to a politician. "Pensacola."

"Never," Malloy said.

"Neither did I."

And then Malloy started to remember what he had so long forgotten: the night in the Miss Texas Club. Out on O Street in Pensacola, all of them drinking Jax beer and eating sardines and cheese crackers; Webb Pierce was singing "There Stands the Glass" on the juke. And then the fight started. One of the rednecks stabbed Rivers, the airplane mechanic, and Sal Costella smashed the guy with the knife and Malloy finished him, and then they all piled in and fought the rednecks—driven by boredom and loneliness, the hands battered, bottles smashing, tables going over, the jukebox wrecked, and then the Shore Patrol came and they fought them too. All except Harrington. Harrington had run.

"I often thought of going back," Harrington said, draining the Scotch and sliding the glass back for a refill. "I bet we wouldn't recognize it."

"Pensacola wouldn't recognize us, either, John."

Harrington laughed a little too loudly, staring straight ahead.

"You're doing good with this movie stuff?" he asked abruptly.

"Well, the government's doing good," Malloy said. "They take all the dough."

Harrington turned slowly. "Why are you living here, anyway? I mean, New York . . . "

"What do you mean?"

"I mean, everyone knows New York is over," Harrington said, his voice full of certainty. "It's a cesspool—"

"It's where I'm from, John," Malloy said. "It's my home. I've tried all the other places."

"But, Jesus, the dirt. The spades. The crime. I don't see how you put up with it. I mean, you don't have to live here, right?"

"That's just the point. I choose to live here."

Harrington smiled. A patronizing smile, Malloy thought, but

what the hell: you couldn't explain the New York thing, you just lived it.

Malloy sipped his beer, remembering. Then, quietly: "Why did you run, John?"

"Run?"

"Yeah."

"What do you mean?"

"That night in the Miss Texas Club, John."

"Oh," Harrington said. "That."

"Yeah, that."

Harrington shrugged. But he did not explain. Doug Ireland came in and he and Malloy talked awhile, and then more people swirled through the revolving door, checking wet coats and umbrellas, and the bar became noisier and more boisterous, an oasis of warmth against the wintry gloom outside. Harrington touched Malloy's elbow.

"Well," he said, "I'll see you, Bobby."

"Yeah," Malloy said. "See you."

"It was nice."

They didn't shake hands. Malloy watched Harrington walk through the crowd to the hatcheck counter. He got his coat and went outside to stand under the awning while a doorman searched the rainy night for a cab. Malloy went to the jukebox. He wanted to hear Webb Pierce. He wanted to hear "There Stands the Glass." Or Hank Williams. Or that girl who sang "Only God Could Make Honky Tonk Angels." He wanted to fight with the Shore Patrol, to be wild and muscled and young. There was no Webb Pierce on the juke. He settled for Tony Bennett. When he looked around, Harrington was gone.

CASEY loved comic books. He had loved them for as long as he could remember, all the way back to World War II, when he would sit at the door at the top of the hall, the spring rain of Brooklyn drumming on the skylight, and read about the Young Allies and The Boy Commandoes and Captain Marvel, Jr. They were his childhood. He could remember nothing else.

"They were sixty-four pages then," he said to me once. "They were fat and thick and only a dime. They were really beautiful."

While soldiers fought the real war, Casey followed Captain America and Bucky as they engaged that most terrible Nazi agent, the Red Skull. Of course, Superman bored him; he was too perfect and Metropolis seemed dull and bright and empty. Batman, on the other hand, lived in New York, a nighttime city of deep shadows, deserted warehouses, speeding cars, pistols, machine guns and cargo hooks, and Casey loved him.

But he also plunged into the world of the Human Torch and his sidekick, Toro, wondering for a long time why the boy's flame was clear and why the Torch was drawn with scratches over his red body. Years later he realized that the scratches were supposed to be muscles. He alternately loved and hated Prince Namor, the Sub-Mariner, who came from the bottom of the sea, the offspring of Princess Fen of Atlantis and an American naval officer. Sometimes Casey would stand on the roof looking out at New York Harbor and wish that he was able, like the Sub-Mariner, to swim that harbor without breathing, for days, weeks, years. Then he would look at the skyscrapers, remembering the epic struggle in that harbor and above those buildings between Sub-Mariner and the Human Torch. It was a draw but Casey knew that Sub-Mariner had the ultimate advantage. He could dive into the sea, where the Torch could not follow. Sometimes Casey wanted to dive into the sea too.

The war ended. For a few more years, his friends would come around in the evening to trade comics. Two without covers for one World's Finest. One Superman for one Archie. Two Archies for one Batman. It was an intricate process full of judgments both aesthetic and moral. But after a while his friends went to high school, graduated, went into the service, got married, moved away. And, of course, they didn't read comics anymore. Casey did. And he saved everything.

He stacked the comics in a white metal cabinet in his room, and when the cabinet was filled, he built shelves that covered all the walls, brought cardboard boxes from Roulston's grocery store and filled them, too, and put them under the bed. The Golden Age had passed: the Torch, Captain America, the Green Lantern, Hawkman, all of them were gone. Superheroes were the first things in his life to go out of style. After a while only Superman and Batman were still being published. Casey started collecting the EC line of comics and became more aware of the work of the artists: the great cinematic drawings of Harvey Kurtzman in *Two-Fisted Tales*; Wally Wood's beautiful renderings of machinery in *Weird Science*; the sense of decomposing bodies evoked by Graham Ingels in *The Haunt of Fear*.

His mother stopped coming into his room to clean. His father called him "the third Collyer brother." And Casey began to feel terribly alone. There was no one to talk to about his passion. In the bars at Coney Island, in places like the Caton Inn, it would have been foolish to speak of Will Eisner's great work in *The Spirit* or how beautifully innocent C. C. Beck had made Captain Marvel. People there were interested in Sugar Ray Robinson and Archie Moore, in politics or the death of Trigger Burke; he wanted to talk about artists like Alex Toth and Roy Crane and Milton Caniff. He ended up talking to himself.

Then the notice came from the Army. Casey had been drafted. The Korean War was over but they needed him anyway, and Casey panicked. If he left the collection behind, his parents would surely throw it out. They just didn't understand. He came to me and asked me to hold everything for him. I was already out of the Navy, living in a place of my own.

"You understand," he said. "You read books. You wouldn't throw books away. These are my books."

Casey was gone two years and I held his collection in seventeen Campbells soup boxes sealed with masking tape. He wrote from time to time, asking about the collection the way some people might ask about their children. He came back with a wife.

She was young and pretty, a California girl who smiled in an amused way when she watched Casey open his collection. "She understands," he whispered to me as they packed the cartons into a U-Haul. They drove away to the house he'd bought in Staten Island with a GI loan. I didn't see him again for almost fifteen years.

I was covering a comic book convention at the old Commodore Hotel one dull Sunday, moving around the racks and tables, looking at the leftover debris of everybody's childhood. Someone called my name. It was Casey. He was older now, bearded and heavier. But behind the rimless glasses, his eyes had a peculiar innocence. In fact, he had eyes like Captain Marvel.

"You'll never believe this," he said. "But I just bought a Noel Sickles original of 'Scorchy Smith' for only three hundred dollars."

He brought me over to a dealer's booth and showed me the strip, which was beautifully drawn, the old Ben Days a rich brown now, giving it the antique glow of a Dutch master. Casey's eyes glazed. I said that it was a beautiful drawing and that I'd always loved Sickles, one of the finest illustrators America has produced.

"My wife will kill me," Casey whispered. "But it's just so goddamned beautiful I had to do it."

He invited me to visit him, and a few weeks later I drove over the Verrazano Bridge to Staten Island. The California girl greeted me at the door. The fresh smile was gone with her youth, her hair was unruly and she had a vacant look in her eyes. She led me inside and shouted to Casey. I heard a typewriter clack, then stop, and Casey came out.

"Sorry," he said, "I was working on my catalog."

And then he gazed around the house, watching for my reaction, as his wife drifted away. There were comics everywhere: all neatly stacked in floor-to-ceiling shelves, individually wrapped in plastic covers, with labels at the bottom of each stack. Planet. Jungle. Daredevil. Marvel.

The walls not covered with shelves were covered with framed

original drawings. A "Terry and the Pirates" by Milton Caniff; a "Captain Easy" by Roy Crane; a "Johnny Hazard" by Frank Robbins; the Sickles; comic book pages by Jack Kirby, Frank Frazetta, Jack Davis, Bernard Krigstein, Bill Everett and others; a Tarzan Sunday page by Burne Hogarth; sports drawings by Willard Mullin and Leo O'Melia, and dozens of others. Buck Rogers ray guns lay on tables, Big Little Books were neatly stacked on one shelf and a bowl contained a collection of buttons, Tom Mix whistling rings, Captain Midnight code-o-graphs. Alone, Casey seemed unbelievably happy. When his wife came back to ask if I wanted tea, he seemed disturbed and self-conscious. When I left, he whispered, "She doesn't understand."

They had no children, except him, and a year later he told me what had finally happened. His wife had saved almost a thousand dollars for a vacation in the Caribbean. It took her almost a year to save the money. But a dealer had called Casey at the insurance company where he worked and told him that an original Hal Foster "Prince Valiant" page had come available for eight hundred dollars. "That," he explained, "was an unbelievable bargain."

Casey agonized. The Foster pages were very difficult to find, and this one contained both the prince and his wife, Aleta, along with a superbly drawn battle on a castle rampart. "I knew I'd never see anything like it again," he said. He took the vacation money out of the bank and bought the page. When he told his wife, she went upstairs, packed her bags in silence and left for California. When she had gone, Casey sat there for a long time, alone again at last.

Then he reached to one of the shelves and took down his copy of Daredevil No. 15. In that one the little fat kid named Meatball has to hide in a dark river to avoid a gang called the Steamrollers. The little fat boy comes out of the river with double pneumonia and dies. Until he read that story years before, Casey had never thought of death. He lay down on the couch and read the book again, remembering the rain on the skylight in Brooklyn, and after a while he fell into the deep, dreamless sleep of a boy.

AF T E R the two oldest children had left for school, Martha sat alone at the large oak table in the kitchen, staring at the front page of the *Times*. The vanished children were still with her, like the dull, insistent throb of a toothache; their hands still touched her, pulled at her, invaded her morning with their presence. The oldest one had slopped the pineapple preserves over everything, and when Martha lifted the *Times* it stuck to the table. The preserves were like the children themselves: sticky, persistent. The difference was that she could not wipe the children away with a damp cloth. She held her breath and waited for the assault of the youngest child, sleeping now in the upstairs room.

She tried to look at the newspaper but the words kept going in and out of focus. A slaughter in Attica. The governor says. Spokesmen said today. Famine threatens Pakistan. She couldn't digest it anymore; the sheer weight of the killing and the misery had canceled the reality behind the words. She could no longer imagine forty people dead at one time. She could not imagine what a famine was like, and besides, the picture of the Cambodian peasant was covered with pineapple preserves. She leaned back, exhausted and drained, and stared at the wall.

She remembered Alec Guinness in *The Horse's Mouth* and how she had spent a year lusting after walls the way Guinness had lusted in the film. She had seen it at the Art Theater on Eighth Street and she tried to figure out the year. She was at Pratt then, so it must have been 1956 or 1957. She had gone to see it with a sculptor who later designed fenders and dashboards for General Motors, telling everyone that design was design and Brancusi would now be working on Buicks. He was a good sculptor and a bad welder and she could not remember his name. She only remembered sleeping with him unhappily at a girlfriend's apartment one night after a loud and raucous party.

From the upper story she heard the youngest child's voice, thin and insistent and demanding. She felt her body stiffen, the throb begin in the lower back, and she tried again to read the *Times*. If she could only ignore the child, if she could wait him out, if she could beat him into silence with indifference, perhaps she could survive. She tried to remember a painting she once did after seeing a show of work by Theodoros Stamos. That was the winter they all wanted to be abstract impressionists. They would go to the Cedar Tavern to look for Franz Kline, whom some of them claimed to have slept with, and on Monday they would start large bold black-and-white paintings, and by Wednesday they would be depressed again. Sitting in the kitchen of the duplex, she wished she could cover over other things with a coat of white.

Indifference collapsed. She went upstairs. She removed the diaper, washed the child, powdered his thin legs and watched him for a long while. Still he cried. There was nothing further she could do for him, yet he demanded something. She lifted him, trying to smother him into silence with her body. Seven months old, and the night he was conceived was as joyless and ordinary as the others.

Holding him, walking down the stairs past the Dubuffet reproductions and the Ben Shahn poster, she thought again about leaving. She had rehearsed it: the note on the oak table, the children left with the neighbor, the walk out the door with clothes in a suitcase. She was always twenty-two in the rehearsal and she was always heading for Paris. She would study French at the Sorbonne and paint in the afternoons, and she remembered the smell of turpentine and linseed oil, remembered the way a palette knife made a flat rough smear on canvas, remembered how well she could draw in the year before everybody decided to become an abstract expressionist. She remembered Gene Kelly's apartment in *An American in Paris*—the bed suspended from the ceiling on pulleys, the easel standing boldly in a corner and north light—and the chimney pots and the pigeons, Gene Kelly's baseball cap and a song called "I'll Build a Stairway to Paradise." She never made it to Paris; she had married instead.

The phone rang. It was her mother, and how are the children, and why don't you come over, and did you hear what happened to Rachel, and how is Sam? Fine, she lied. Fine. Everything is fine. Just fine. Fine, fine, fine. And when she finished, the baby still glued to her, she started to cry. She couldn't leave, couldn't bear the thought of Sam's grave lawyer's face as he stared at her empty closet or went to retrieve the children as if they were strays at the pound. She would sit here and wait.

She went over to the stove and started heating a bottle for the baby, and after a while she put him into the playpen. Then she opened the *Times* and turned to the back and looked at the weather report. It was fifty-eight and sunny in Paris, and she thought that maybe in a week she would paint the walls.

O N New Year's Eve, my friend Henry Bail always stayed home. There were just too many drunks abroad: college boys drowned in beer; kids from Jersey with their fathers' cars; biology teachers full of Old Overholt; bosses with secretaries; Dutch sailors; off-duty Westchester cops; financial writers. Henry Bail despised them all. They were amateurs. They drove cars like maniacs. They always wanted to fight.

"I stay home," he said to me year after year. "I have a special pair of pajamas I wear for the occasion. Silk jobs. I put on a robe over the pajamas. I put on a real good pair of slippers. I order a good dinner, catered, you know. From Zabar's or some Chinese joint. I lay it all out. I listen to music. Something calm and dumb. Ravel. Something like that. I open a bottle of wine. Not champagne. I can't stand that stuff. But something good. I eat. I drink the wine. I lie on the couch. Around a quarter to twelve I put on the TV. I watch Guy Lombardo. They do 'Auld Lang Syne' and then I turn it off. I go to bed. I read awhile and I listen to all the car crashes and wonder how they get the bodies back to Jersey."

Henry Bail, of course, lived alone. He used to quote Henry Higgins, describing himself as "a confirmed old bachelor, and likely to remain so." Actually, at forty-three he wasn't so old and he wasn't gay. He just didn't like the clutter of a marriage: the extra things in the bathroom; the crowded closets; the steady pressure to entertain someone else every day and to talk when you wanted silence.

"I tried that marriage thing once," he would say, with a dark chuckle, "and found out I didn't have a talent for it. When you're married, nothing is ever the same when you come home. Someone moves the book. Someone eats the lemon in the fridge. It's always different. Someone else's fingerprints are everywhere. And when

I was married, New Year's was the worst. You make a resolution and there's always someone around to nag you when you break it."

Henry Bail always made the same New Year's resolutions. He would stop smoking. He would go to the gym and lose weight and get the heart pumping again. He would read all of Balzac. He'd take a real vacation, with no work in the briefcase. Henry Bail loved making resolutions.

"I never keep any of them," he said. "That's why I make them. I know what I am *supposed* to do and then I just do what I *want* to do. I guess I'm what the shrinks call a highly developed egotist. Or maybe I just like sin. Sin is what you're not supposed to do. A wife doesn't like you to sin."

Last New Year's Eve he had just stepped out of a long soak in the bath and was pulling on his silk pajamas when the phone rang. He picked it up, thinking it was me calling for his list of resolutions. It wasn't me.

"Hello, Henry." His heart sank. "It's Helen."

Helen was Henry Bail's first and only wife, and he had not heard from her for eight years. The alimony checks went out every month and they were cashed, but he didn't stay in touch. They had no children and Henry Bail didn't feel anything for her except indifference.

He knew that she had lived in Mexico for a while, studying watercolor painting; she had gone to Europe, to Biarritz, Rome, Lausanne. She apparently lived well. She apparently took lovers. But Henry Bail did not resent the alimony that paid for all this. He had learned his lesson and alimony was the price.

"I need help, Henry. I don't know who to call except you."

"Helen, I . . . I'm in my pajamas and—"

"I've got to see you," she said. "It's important. It really is. If it wasn't, I wouldn't have called. Have I ever called you for help before?"

"No, you haven't, Helen. But—"

"Please." There was a perfect tremor of need, helplessness and despair in her voice. Henry Bail sighed. He asked her where she was and she gave him an address on Morton Street in the Village; he said that he was all the way up on the West Side and asked if it could wait, and she said no, it couldn't. So Henry Bail got dressed, bade farewell to his catered dinner and went out on New Year's Eve.

"It took me twenty minutes to find a cab," Henry said later. "The driver was a lunatic hippie who apologized for the smell when I got in. Two Frenchmen had thrown up in the back on their way to Harlem. He had picked them up at '21.' I asked him if he knew what they'd ordered and he laughed and drove me to Morton Street in about four minutes."

Two transvestites, dressed as Joan Crawford and Bette Davis, were singing "Yesterday" on the corner of Seventh Avenue when he stepped out of the cab. He passed a middle-aged man in a velvet-collared coat sleeping against a fence, and hurried up the stoop of Helen's house. There was another name on the bell of the apartment she had given him, but he rang the buzzer anyway.

"I couldn't believe it when I saw her," he said. "She was over two hundred pounds and looked twenty years older than me. She was sitting in the living room of this place, which she borrowed from some friend who was away for the holidays. I hardly recognized her."

She locked the door behind him, offered Bail a drink and, when he turned her down, poured a stiff one for herself. When she sat down in a leather chair, her body made a squashing sound. Bail tried to remember the women he had almost married before he met Helen: the conga player from the Bronx; the French Canadian woman with an infant son; the publicist from Elmhurst. Now, as then, Helen crowded all of them off the stage. Helen was here in front of him.

"What is it, Helen?" he said. "What do you need?"

"I don't know how to ask."

"Helen," he said, "I want to go home and get in bed and watch Guy Lombardo—"

"Okay," she said. "I need twenty-five thousand dollars."

"Mother of mercy!"

"If I don't get twenty-five grand," she said, "somebody is going to break my legs."

"Who?"

"Some people. Believe me, they'll do it."

She told Henry Bail part of her story: she was enticed into gambling in Europe by an Austrian ball-bearing manufacturer; got in deeper while accompanying an oil sheik from Yemen around the various watering holes; busted out with a British movie producer in Monte Carlo and woke up one morning to find herself a degenerate gambler.

"I got back to New York four months ago," she told him. "I borrowed from certain people to pay off some other people. Now these people want their money back, Henry. And I don't have any money. I have minus money, Henry. I could die."

It briefly occurred to Henry that he would save more than fifteen hundred a month in alimony if she did die; he could buy good prints with that money, and wine, and rare editions of books. But as he rose from his chair and stared at the usual Klimt reproduction, and as a picture formed of poor Helen lying in an alley with her legs at right angles to each other, Henry Bail felt the first stirring of that most treacherous of emotions, pity.

"I tried to fight it off," he said later. "But there was something about her voice that reminded me of the fat girl at the dance watching everybody else do the samba."

Bail lectured her sternly, made her swear she would join Gamblers Anonymous, told her she must see a shrink. And then he told her to call his accountant when the holiday was over.

As he rose to leave, she was grateful in the most terrifying way: she cried, she sobbed, she hugged him in her huge, thick arms, she asked him if he wanted to stay the night. Henry Bail was fond of the fleshy maidens painted by Rubens, but not that fond. He shook her hand, wished her a happy New Year and went out into the night.

"The guy with the velvet-collared coat was still leaning against the fence when I went out," he remembered, "except his pockets had been cut open and were hanging down like flaps. Another transvestite, dressed like Farrah Fawcett, came down the block dribbling a basketball and singing 'Over the Rainbow.' There were no cabs. No cabs at all. It was freezing. I walked up to Sheridan Square.

"Two guys with funny hats were stomping a third guy with a funny hat in front of Smiler's. The special cop inside was busy checking whether people were carrying out quarter pounds of butter stuck in a *Daily News.* I asked one of the funny hats why he was stomping the guy on the sidewalk. He punched me in the eye. When I could see again, all three of them were gone.

"I walked uptown. At St. Vincent's two women were lugging a guy out of a cab. His face was covered with blood. I ran to the cab but it sped away, I guess in terror. I could barely see out of my eye and I hadn't felt my own fingers for the last four blocks. I tried to remember the symptoms of frostbite and whether you soaked your feet in hot or cold water."

At Fourteenth Street he crossed the avenue to avoid three young men who were playing Three Musketeers with switchblades; he stepped over the inert body of a marine; a shopping-bag lady was huddled in a doorway, moaning, but Henry Bail kept going, cursing the large woman who was once his wife. Suddenly it was midnight.

Windows opened. Tin horns blew. Up ahead was Times Square, teeming with maniacs. He started down into the subway at Twenty-third Street, thought he saw a guy at the token booth with a gun, turned around and started to run. He heard Guy Lombardo's greatest hit playing from an open window. Two middle-aged men tumbled out of a saloon, hitting each other with bottles. Henry Bail hurried east to avoid Times Square and Eighth Avenue, and outside Macy's he found a cab that would take him home.

"When I got there, I fell into bed and lay there for a while, just shaking," he told me. "When I fell asleep, I didn't dream."

His black eye lingered for ten days. He arranged to give Helen the twenty-five thousand dollars, to be paid off at the rate of one hundred dollars a month out of her alimony for the next twenty years or so. After she cashed the check, Helen left town without a word of thanks. The woman who rented the apartment on Morton Street said she thought Helen had gone to Las Vegas. But Henry Bail was not bitter.

"After all," he said to me, "I'm alive."

This year I called him for his resolutions. But Henry Bail wasn't answering the phone.

E V E R Y year when the calendar started moving toward St. Patrick's Day, Malloy remembered the stranger who long ago had come to the old neighborhood in Brooklyn.

Malloy was twelve then, working after school in Roulston's grocery store on the corner of Eleventh Street and Seventh Avenue. His father had been dead a year and this was the boy's first job. And one afternoon at the end of winter, he looked up from the cellar of the store, where he was unloading soup boxes, and saw him.

The stranger was on the other side of the avenue, walking in a tight, rolling swagger, the collar of his camel's-hair coat pulled up to his chin, a pearl-gray broadbrim hat riding low on his brow, his polished pointed shoes jutting out from pegged pants. He was carrying a small leather bag, the kind that fighters used when they went to the gym, and he was looking at the numbers of the houses, obviously searching for an address.

He stopped a few doors past Rattigan's Bar and Grill and went into the hallway between Bernsley's Heating and Appliance and the variety store. He did not come back out again.

That night when his mother came home from work, Bobby told her about this stranger who was dressed like a vaguely sinister character in a movie he had seen once at the Minerva. She sipped her steaming tea, piling in the sugar, and told Bobby that if his father were still alive, they would find out soon enough about this stranger. But now they'd have to wait until the man revealed himself to all of them.

"He never came out again," he said. "Where do you think he went?"

"Old Kate Flanagan on the second floor still rents rooms," his mother said. "He's probably up there in one of them. Probably just a new worker for the factory."

But the stranger did not come out of the building the next day, nor the day after that. He was not a worker in the factory. Not in those clothes. At night Bobby Malloy would stare at the drawn shades of the tenement across the street, looking at the second floor where Kate Flanagan kept rooms. The man never showed himself.

Then, eight days after the man arrived, Bobby Malloy was washing the windows and saw a shade go up across the street. The stranger was sitting there. He wore a black shirt buttoned at the wrists and his chin was a pale blue. He sat back from the window, so you could not see him easily from the street. At dusk he pulled the shade down again.

A few days later, Bobby was carrying a case of peaches up from the cellar of Roulston's. When he went into the store, the stranger was at the counter. Bobby froze.

The stranger seemed to feel the boy's eyes on him. He turned and looked at him with bright-blue penetrating eyes. The boy smiled nervously; the man nodded, lifted his groceries and went out. For the next few weeks, Bobby saw him sitting at the window, smoking Camels, reading newspapers. He had a radio, and when Bobby walked under the window one afternoon, he could hear Red Barber announcing the Dodger game. The man spent his days like that. Waiting. But Bobby never saw him in the store again.

One warm Friday night, the boy's mother worked late and he went down to the street to hang out until she came home. He was sitting on the stoop of the glazier's shop when he first saw the Packard. The car was long, black and highly polished. There were two men inside. The car moved slowly along the avenue, turned up Twelfth Street and disappeared. A few minutes later it came down Eleventh Street and turned onto the avenue, moving slowly and deliberately. After the Packard came around for the third time and vanished up Twelfth Street, Bobby Malloy ran across the street and into the house where the stranger was staying. His heart was pounding.

He rapped swiftly on the stranger's door. Nobody answered. He knocked again and heard someone shift in a bed.

"Hello in there," Bobby said. "It's me, from the grocery store. I gotta talk to you."

A key turned slowly in the lock. The door jerked open suddenly and Bobby jumped back. The stranger was standing in his
shorts, a gun in his hand.

"Jesus Christ," the stranger sighed. "You almost got your
head blowed off, kid."

"I'm sorry," Bobby Malloy said, looking at the gun; it was the
color of old nickels. "But I had to tell you. There's a long black car,
a Packard, I think, went around the block three times now.
There's two guys inside."

The stranger glanced at the drawn window shades and
squinted at Bobby Malloy, but he didn't say anything.

"They looking for you?" the boy asked.

"Nah."

The stranger went to the bureau and came back with a dollar.
"Thanks, kid," he said. "And listen, you didn't see anything up
here, right?"

"Right."

"Go home and do your homework," the stranger said. And
Malloy went home.

St. Patrick's Day was two days later. For those two days he
saw neither the stranger nor the Packard. And on St. Patrick's
Day he marched with his school, full of band music and the sound
of the drums bouncing defiantly off the walls of Fifth Avenue.
When he came home, the doors of Rattigan's were wide open to
the spring air and he could hear the men singing the old songs.
The ones his father used to sing. He took a book from upstairs and
sat on a cellar board under a street lamp. The weather turned
cold. The door of the bar closed. He looked up at the stranger's
room; the shade was still drawn.

It was almost nine o'clock before he saw his mother come up
out of the subway three blocks away. There were two men with
her and she was walking funny. He started to walk to her when
he saw one of the men push her hard.

She fell awkwardly against the window of the bakery and
then swung her handbag at the man. The other one shoved her
again. Malloy dropped his book and started to run. He dived at the
first one, a large red-faced man who looked Irish and had a sour
smell on his rough clothes.

"For the love of God, Robert, don't . . . " his mother said. But the man slammed the boy against the door of a barbershop. Bobby fell like an injured toy.

"Lousy Irish bitch," the second one said, and then the two of them were shoving at her. The boy tried to get up, hearing muffled Irish music playing behind the shuttered doors of Rattigan's, a block away. His mother's voice was slurred and choked: "I didn't promise nothin' . . . " Bobby got up and the first one knocked him down again. He remembered later how he had felt nothing, how the sidewalk just came up and hit him in the face.

And suddenly there was a whirl of kicking and movement, and Bobby looked up and saw the stranger.

The stranger hit the second man in the face, turned him and came back savagely with his elbow, smashing him in the jaw. Something broke. The man fell. The first one threw a wild right hand and hit the stranger in the face. Bobby Malloy had never seen a man so terrible as the stranger was after that first punch. The stranger whipped off the camel's-hair coat, moved at the bigger man with his chin tucked low and ripped a volley of punches to the man's belly. The big man wheezed and grabbed at him, but he backed off, drove a vicious hook into the man's kidneys and then stopped the man from falling by hitting him on the chin with his right hand.

Then the stranger shoved him against the wall with the left hand, pinning him, and hit him again and again with the right.

"No more!" Malloy's mother said. "For God's sake, no more!"

The stranger let the big man slide down the wall into a sitting position, bent forward at the waist, his face a smear.

"Son of a bitch," the stranger said. He flicked dust off his jacket, looked at the two fallen men and went over and picked up his camel's-hair coat. The door of Rattigan's opened and some of the men stepped out.

"We were at the parade," Malloy's mother said hoarsely. "They said . . . they said they would take me home. I thought we'd just go for a drink, but no, they wanted more."

The stranger gave her a look.

"Can I buy *you* a drink at least?" she said. "For St. Patty's Day?"

"Nah," he said. "I'm Italian."

He smiled thinly at Bobby Malloy, nodded and then moved off quickly along the avenue, away from Rattigan's, looking over his shoulder at the traffic as if expecting the arrival of the Packard. He hurried down the steps to the subway. Bobby Malloy knew he would never see him again, and he was right.

HANLON woke up on Sunday morning and peeked through the blinds, and the snow was still falling. The night before, the radio had predicted snow turning to rain but it was still snowing; the cars on his block were covered, and when he opened the window an inch, he could hear tire chains and the protesting wheeze of the Seventh Avenue bus. He reached for the phone and called the girl, but again there was no answer. There had been no answer since before Christmas.

He called his answering service, and there were two calls from movie people in California but nothing from the girl. He turned on the radio and listened to Jonathan Schwartz on WNEW. Halfway through shaving, he heard Dinah Washington singing "Just Friends," and he wanted to go back to sleep forever.

Just friends, the song said, *lovers no more. Just friends, not like before* . . . He called again, thinking that maybe she had been asleep, had turned off the phone, had gone out for the paper. The phone rang six times and Hanlon hung up. Then he called me.

"Meet me for breakfast," he said. "At the Purity."

"I have a column to write today, Hanlon, and—"

"In half an hour," he said. "I'm desperate."

Hanlon dressed and called his service to give them the number of the Purity Diner, in case she called, and then he went out into the snow. He was sitting in a booth along the wall when I showed up.

"I can't get her on the phone," Hanlon said bleakly.

"Who?"

"The girl I'm in love with. The one you met at the Village Gate that night we saw Stanley Turrentine. The dark one with the terrific smile. The public relations one."

"The kid?"

"She's not that young," Hanlon said lamely. The waitress came over and we ordered eggs and coffee. "She's twenty-six," he said, picking it up again. "But she's an old twenty-six, you know what I mean? Mature . . . she knows a lot of things I don't know."

"Like what?" I asked. "The name of each member of Kiss? What good is that? You're forty-one, Hanlon. Does she know who Sandy Amoros was? Does she remember Augie Galan? Can she tell you who the catcher was before Roy Campanella? Does she know how many bases Maynard DeWitt stole at Montreal in 1948? What does she really know, Hanlon?"

"She knows plenty," Hanlon said. The waitress brought the eggs and coffee. He looked at them glumly.

"Well, she certainly knows how to turn you into a basket case. Where did you meet this dame?"

"We met cute," he said, "in the ladies' sweater department at Bloomingdale's. I was trying to buy a sweater for my daughter and she was there, and I asked her if she knew sizes and I described my daughter and she picked out the size. Then I asked her if she felt like having a frozen hot chocolate and she said sure, so we went up the block to Serendipity."

"I always bump my head on the lamps in that joint," I said. "Anyway, then what happened?"

"One thing led to another. She was handling some punk rock group called Blue Acne or something and she invited me to come hear them. Why not? I went to see them. They were terrible. The usual suburban jerks trying to act like tough guys in the big city, playing the usual two chords on the guitar, very loudly. I told her I thought they stunk. She agreed. So I took her over to the Gate to see Turrentine. She never heard anything like that before."

"At least that's what she told you," I said.

"Yeah."

He started to see her two or three nights a week, usually too late for a movie because of her job, but early enough to listen to music. They saw Dizzy Gillespie at the Gate, Max Roach at the Vanguard, Dexter Gordon at Carnegie Hall, Ellis Larkins at the Carnegie Tavern, Jimmie Rowles at Bradley's. He bought her the collection of John Cheever's stories; he took her to eat at the River Cafe, under the Brooklyn Bridge, and rented a car one weekend so he could show her Sheepshead Bay and Coney Island.

"She seemed to love it. She's from Cleveland and I was showing her another world, you know?"

"Like a tour guide?" I asked. "Or an archeologist?"

"Both." Clearly, Hanlon was going through the stages described by Stendhal: admiration, delight, hope, followed by "crystallization . . . that process of the mind which discovers fresh perfections in its beloved at every turn of events." The result is love. I mentioned this to him.

"Well, that's what happened," he said. "And right away I started to worry. It was all right when I first met her. But when I fell in love with her, I started to worry. I worried I was too old. I worried I didn't have enough money, with the alimony payments and all. I worried that she thought I was just a big dummy."

"Stendhal lists that as the sixth stage: doubt," I said. We finished the eggs and the waitress brought us more coffee. The snow had turned at last to rain and the diner was getting crowded. "You were right on schedule."

"Christmas did me in," Hanlon said. "There were a couple of parties I wanted her to go to with me. She couldn't, she was working. Then I pinned her down one night and brought her some Christmas presents. She thanked me but she seemed embarrassed because she didn't have anything for me. I didn't care. I just wanted her to love me." That night they went to eat at Billy's on First Avenue, and by the time they reached the coffee, Hanlon was asking her to marry him.

"She was really nice," he said. "She held my hand. She kissed me on the cheek. She said it was an honor. But she never answered the question. All the way home, I knew I'd made a mistake. I should've been more cool. I should have just shut up." He stirred his black coffee. "I haven't been able to get her on the phone since that night."

"So forget her, Hanlon," I said. "You probably scared her to death. She probably sees you as a nice old busted valise, which is what you and I are, Hanlon. Let's face it. But don't let it get you down. There's a thousand women in this town."

"She's the only one I want," he said.

"Forget her. She probably ran off with a trombone player or something. Maybe she became a nun."

"That's why I called you," he said. "I knew you'd listen with your usual compassion and delicacy and tact."

"Always glad to help."

Then the waitress came down the aisle calling Hanlon's name. He rose from the booth, his face trembling, and followed her to the telephone. He was gone less than a minute. When he came back, his face looked like a sunrise.

"That was her," he said. "She was in Aruba for a rest and just got back and she wants to see me. Right now. Today. This afternoon." He pulled on his coat. "I'll see you, chump."

"Hey, what about the check?" I said.

"Put it on my bill," Hanlon said, and he walked out into the rain. I had another cup of coffee and then went to the phone and called a woman I know. I let it ring six times but she wasn't home.

T H E Y called her Big Red from the day that she first showed up at the Copa, in the spring of 1949. She was nineteen years old then, with clean peach-colored skin, legs that started at her rib cage and a mane of flaming red hair that made grown men walk into lampposts. On that first day Jules Podell, who ran the place, didn't even rap his pinkie ring against a table when he saw her or scream from the darkness of the banquettes or demand an audition. He took one look at the hair and the legs and the skin and he hired her on the spot.

And for a year Big Red was one of the glories of New York. The waiters loved her; the dishwashers politely bowed their hellos; and Frank Costello, when he came around, always called her Miss Red.

Her secret was a kind of clumsy innocence. Big Red couldn't dance much, although she could kick her legs higher than her chin; her voice was as frail as a sparrow in traffic; she didn't go to acting classes, didn't dream of a niche in the Hollywood solar system. She was just a great big girl who bumped into things—doors, waiters and other dancers—and was always forgiven because she was so beautiful and so nice.

Podell, who usually punished his enemies by screaming them deaf, never raised his voice to her. And the hoodlums protected her. Whenever an armed citizen visiting from Detroit would try to drag her into the Burma Road, a dim purgatory of seats against the back wall, he would be strongly advised to lay off. Big Red was different. Big Red went to grammar school in a convent. Big Red was a nice girl.

"I want the red-headed broad," one underwear buyer shouted one night. "I'd like to give her a boff."

"If ya open ya mout about da red-headed broad again," said

a gentleman in an elegant sharkskin suit, "you will never talk for da rest of ya life."

A few such choice words usually settled the matter, although it was rumored that several citizens, including the pudgy son of a Caribbean dictator, had to be deposited with force on the cement of East Sixtieth Street before they got the point.

Then Sal came into her life. Sal was from Bensonhurst and he was only five foot four and twenty-one years old. He had clean, perfect features, like a wonderful miniature painting, and he wanted to be a singer. Well, not just a singer. He wanted to be Frank Sinatra.

He came to audition one day and stood next to a piano, held a cigarette in his right hand and loosened the bow tie of his rented tux with his left. He sang "This Love of Mine," "I'll Never Be the Same," "Just One of Those Things" and "Nancy, With the Laughing Face." He was tender like Frank and he swaggered like Frank and he bent the notes the way Frank did, holding the high ones and reaching down into the lower register when he was hurting the most. Just like Frank.

But in those years, the Copacabana already had one Frank Sinatra. The real one. They didn't need another, particularly one who was only slightly taller than a mailbox. So Julie Podell told the kid to grow six inches and learn to sing like himself and in the meantime he should try *The Ted Mack Amateur Hour,* maybe he could get work at the RKO Prospect in Brooklyn. Sal was destroyed.

He walked out of the frigid darkness of the club into the warm afternoon air just as Big Red was arriving for a rehearsal. Big Red bumped into him, almost knocking him down, and then realized that tears were streaming down his face.

"Oh, you poor little thing," Big Red said. "You're gonna get your tuxedo wet."

That started it. She put her long arms around him and hugged him, and he leaned into her largeness, and she patted his head and told him everything was going to be all right—don't you worry, Sal, everything'll be fine. And for a while it was. Three days later Sal moved into Big Red's place in Chelsea, and when she wasn't working they went everywhere together. She had the money from the Copa; he had his dream.

But as the months went by, Sal started going a little crazy. His pride started to eat away at his brain; would Frank Sinatra let a girl pay the bills? Would Frank let his girl work every night half-naked in front of a bunch of drunks? Big Red woke up one day about noon and saw Sal looking out the kitchen window into the backyard. His body was shaking as if he couldn't control his laughter. She smiled, tiptoed over to him and leaned down to kiss him on the head, and then realized that he was crying.

It all came pouring out: the bruised pride, the sense of being a leech or worse, his need to make it on his own. And he told her he wanted to go to Vegas, where Bugsy Siegel had built the Flamingo and where a lot of new joints were opening up. He was sure he could get work there as a singer. He was sure he could get the big break. All he needed was enough money for a car and the trip west. He was sure he could get the money from an uncle on Eighty-sixth Street and Fourteenth Avenue. And he wanted Big Red to go with him.

So Big Red gave her notice, and that was the closest anyone had ever come to seeing Jules Podell cry. He sat there like a museum director who had just lost the "Mona Lisa." That Saturday night all the regulars gave Big Red a farewell party after the last show. The hoodlums were there too, looking sad. They gave her phone numbers in Vegas, certain well-connected parties to call. And they gave her a necklace, a set of luggage and a big cake, among other things.

But when she went outside carrying all the gifts, Sal was not there waiting as he was supposed to be. Sal was in the squad room of a police station in Brooklyn, and two homicide cops were typing up forms charging him with murder. Sal had borrowed a gun and walked into a saloon to get the money for the Vegas trip. There was a fight, the gun had gone off and a bartender was dead. Sal was on his way to Attica.

A few days later one of the Copa regulars called Big Red. One of the hoodlums. He told her Sal would be gone for a long time. She was welcome to come back to the Copa, but when she said no, that the Copa would only remind her of Sal, this party said that an airline ticket to Vegas would be waiting for her at Idlewild. And a job would be waiting for her when she got there. She cried for two days and then went west. She never heard a word from Sal.

She worked at the Dunes and did the Lido de Paris show for a couple of years; she married and divorced an Oklahoma oil man, then married a beauty parlor operator who later died in a car crash. Her three children grew up, went to school, married, went away. She settled in Santa Monica in a small house two blocks from the Pacific. She planted a garden, watched TV, talked a lot to her children on the phone and started going to Mass. Every day, to stay in shape, she spent an hour in the ocean.

One morning she came back from the beach and the phone was ringing. The operator asked her name and said she had a person-to-person call from New York.

"Okay, that's me. Go ahead, Operator."

"I have your party on the line," the operator said in a metallic voice.

"Oh, great, great, Operator, thank you. Thanks."

The voice was familiar.

"It's me, Sal," the voice said. "They just let me out."

She turned around quickly, bumped into the table and knocked the toaster to the floor.

"Sal? That's really you, Sal?"

"Yeah. I been tryin' for three days to find a number for you. I called everywheres. Vegas. Texas. Julie Podell's dead, you know?"

"Yeah, I heard that, Sal."

"I must've missed it somehow. I didn't know it. New York sure ain't the same, is it?"

"I guess not. That was too bad about Julie."

"Hey, listen, I gotta ask you something."

"Yeah, Sal?"

"Are you married?"

"No."

She could hear him breathe out hard in relief. "Well, I'd like to come out there," he said. "I'd like to get a job out there, start over."

There was a long pause. "I don't look the way I used to look," she said, her voice trembling.

"Neither do I," Sal said, his voice dropping into the lower register.

"I've got grown-up kids and all. I have a garden. I even go to church. I'm really boring."

"So am I."

"Uh, when were you, uh, thinking of coming out?"

"Tonight," he said.

"Tonight?" She turned, tangled in the phone wire and reached for the toaster. She knocked over a chair. "Uh, well, gee, that'd be . . . What flight?"

He gave her the number. She wrote it on the wall beside the phone.

"I'll be there," she said. "I'll be at the gate. I'll be wearing, uh, black slacks and a white blouse. I'll be there, Sal. I'll be there. I'm big, remember? With red hair."

She hung up, stood still there for a moment and then kicked a leg higher than her chin.

ALL winter Levinsky waited for the snow. At night, lying with Sandra in the apartment on Bank Street, he would stare out at the blue-black sky, cursing the stars and longing for storms and whiteness. But it was a winter empty of snow. And so he would lie there and try to explain the snow to her, this long Florida girl who had chosen, incredibly, to love him.

"The best one of all was in 1947," he said. "It snowed for two days and the backyards were filled up, right to the fences. You couldn't open the doors to the roofs, they were so piled up with snow. Traffic stopped, the trolleys didn't run—"

"Trolleys?"

"They were these long electric cars, with a thing on the back that connected to electric power lines. Sort of shaped like railroad trains . . . I don't know, a trolley is hard to explain."

And so was the snow: the chimneys helmeted by the snow; a cat moving across the white blanket; the silence falling on Brooklyn as the traffic vanished; and the snow squeaking when you walked. In 1947 there were mountains of snow on all the corners, and the kids carved ice tunnels into their white hearts and made noises to each other like Eskimos. Sandra: golden girl: he could not explain these things to her, or Livonia Avenue either.

"It doesn't matter," she would say whenever he tried in his fumbling way to explain himself or his life. And to Levinsky that was the beautiful part. She loved Levinsky! Incredible! The details did not matter. She loved Levinsky, who had always been too short for the women he desired; Levinsky, who had moved into his thirties bursting with love and no one to give it to; Levinsky, who poured his energies into the shirt business, who was kind to his employees, but who ate too many dinners alone, watched too many late shows and could not make it with hookers anymore.

And then Sandra had arrived. She answered a model call one day, asked him to buy her dinner because she was starving and went home with him that night and stayed. As simple as that. She filled his place in the Village with flowers, a huge brass pot they bought in the Hamptons, an antique wooden pepper grinder, record albums, framed prints, books and more. It was the more that made Levinsky glow through the days at the office, the sense of feminine merger she brought to his life: cosmetics, perfumes, oils, mysterious tubes, powders, hair conditioners and lotions crowded the top of his once-barren dresser; the bureau drawers were filled with stockings, panties, filmy things; in the closet dresses hung like joyous multicolored skins among his somber suits. All of it feeding Levinsky's astonished heart.

And now, on this February afternoon at the office, he even had the snow. He said goodnight to everyone and went out onto Twenty-eighth Street and started walking to the Village. The snow was falling in huge wet flakes; he skimmed a finger over the snow gathered on the hood of a car and knew that it would pack well, that it would stick. Beautiful. She had never seen New York under snow and it reminded him again that he had known her for only three months, that he had already asked her to marry him, just two nights before. He had trembled when he asked her; she was fifteen years younger, after all, and a *shiksa* at that. But she smiled, she didn't say no. Maybe the snow was all he needed.

It was dark when he reached Bank Street, and as he made the turn he started packing a snowball from the snow on top of a Buick. When he reached the house, he threw the snowball up at the second-floor window. And then he realized that the apartment was dark. A wire of panic moved through him as he rushed up the stairs.

"Sandra?" he called, stepping into the living room. The huge Leonard Baskin print was gone from over the fireplace and the Cuevas was missing from the wall beside the bookcase where she had hung it. The brass pot was gone and the paper flowers, and there were black slots in the bookcases and gashes in the rows of record albums. In the bedroom her bureau was empty, and a card lay on top of the barren dresser. "Love. Understand. And thanks. Sandra."

He felt the sound moving up from inside him before he heard it: deep, animal, wounded. He moved frantically around the bedroom, opening drawers, looking behind the dresser, opening the closet. His suits hung neatly but she was gone. He tore at the suits, pulling them to the floor, hurled the neckties across the room and ripped at the slacks until he saw a single dress, yellow and summery, hanging in solitude behind a raincoat. He lifted it gently, feeling the fabric. And then he held it to himself, embracing it, feeling fat and ugly and old beside it; he fell back on the bed, crying out his injury and his loss. After a while he could cry no more. And he lay very still, watching the snow fall through the dark night.

W

H E N the telephone rang in the kitchen, Rhinelander was deep in the leather chair beside the living room window, drowsy with dinner, reading Liddell Hart's history of the Second World War. His cigar had burned halfway down, and on the second ring he shifted from the raid on Dieppe to the lights of Queens that shone through the rain across the dark river. He tapped away an ash and was aware of his wife as she moved to the phone; heard her murmuring voice, but not the words; heard the dull plastic sound of the receiver returning to its cradle, and shortly felt her beside him. She stood for a moment in silence before touching his arm. Her touch was cold.

"That was your daughter," she said, then paused. "Margaret's dead. She died twenty minutes ago, in the hospital."

"Oh my God." The book fell but he didn't move. "Oh my God."

"She wants you to come over there."

"Yes," Rhinelander said. "Of course I'll go. Margaret—my God."

"Do you want me to drive?" his wife asked.

"No. I'll go alone."

The traffic was sluggish with the rain, and as he stopped on Third Avenue for a light, he began counting, starting with the birthday so carefully observed for the eleven years of their marriage. She was only forty-seven, he thought. Oh my God.

Heading west, he drove into the park at the Sixty-sixth Street transverse. The rain was pounding down now, battering the spring trees, running in small rivers along the curb. And he remembered a night long ago when they had lain in the park's damp grass, staring at the New York sky. That night they furnished houses, conceived children, imagined all sorts of triumphs. There would be a train set for their son, a piano for their daughter and an *Encyclopaedia Britannica,* yes, an encyclopedia: all the things he had never had himself in the tight Depression alleys of Brownsville. She had added softness to the plans, a promise of kindness and a sense of duration. And later they had gone down to Fifty-seventh Street and taken a room at the Great Northern Hotel, and made shy and furious love until morning.

"I was twenty-one," Rhinelander said out loud. "She was eighteen."

The West Side Highway was closed, so he drove through Harlem to the bridge for Jersey. And he remembered how it was later, after it was over: he had left their apartment and she had learned to punish him.

"Be civilized," he once said to her. But she had smiled coldly and refused to answer. She chose instead to live her grand refusal, never to remarry, never even to live with another man. She embraced maternal duty and self-sacrifice, Rhinelander thought, the way some religious people embrace self-flagellation, loving her children as a means of damning him.

The car seemed to be driving him now, pulling him across the bridge into Jersey, along roads that to him had always meant pain. He wondered how many hours he had spent driving those roads with the kids when they were young, feeding them at Howard Johnson's, searching for picnic spots, trying in some stiff, agonized way to let them know he was there because he wanted to be there. And later he would take them home and they would wave from the door of the silent house.

He shook off the past and focused on the details of the present. There must be insurance; he had paid it himself for most of her life. And there would be a plot of land somewhere for burial, and he assumed that even as he drove, her body was on its way to a funeral home . . .

Her body: the way her hair turned gold in the summer sun, bleached out and very fine on her arms, and how he loved to watch her walk along the beach, the skin taut, the muscles of her legs long and firm. He remembered telling her once, long ago, that they would make love in all the great cities of the world, that they would fill shelves with used-up passports and always, always come home. But they had only one passport together, and he wondered whether she had saved it, as she had so many other things—letters, a wedding gown, photographs—as iron proof of her endurance.

Quite suddenly he was on her street. The rain had stopped and he sat for a moment, inhaling the dark, rich smell of the night. His oldest daughter's car, with Massachusetts plates, was parked in the driveway. A dog barked in the distance. The upstairs bedroom was brightly lit, and Rhinelander looked at it for a long moment, wondering whether it had ever been filled with delight and hope and possibility, whether, just once, someone else had told her sweet lies there about the great cities of the world. Then he got out of the car and crossed the street, wishing that just once, before it ended, he had found the time to tell her that he loved her.

TH E two Chinese men lived in the first house around the corner from us in the old neighborhood in Brooklyn. We lived on the top floor of one of the tenements on the avenue. We had no backyard. Instead, we looked straight down from our kitchen window into the yard of the Chinese men, which pushed in at a right angle from the side street.

Their yard was a jungle. Wild weed trees climbed fifteen feet into the air, angling across one another, reaching for sunlight that was blocked by the walls of a garage. Skunkweed and thorn bushes fought each other for space. The tangled grass was three feet high, spreading to the wall of the house. At dusk we could see the eyes of cats gleaming in the mauve light, threading through the high grass. But the door to the house was always closed and the blackout shades drawn tight. We never saw the Chinese men in the yard.

Sometimes the taller one would come into Roulston's, the grocery store on the corner, where I worked as a delivery boy. He was always dressed in a blue serge suit that was shiny in the pants and he always ordered the same thing: Luckies and quart bottles of beer. He never bought anything else and he never had anything delivered.

The other man was shorter and he wore a gray sweater under his suit jacket, even in summer. He had thick black-rimmed glasses and a crew cut. In that neighborhood—Irish and Italian, with a scattering of Jews—the Chinese men were absolute strangers. They did not go to our churches. They didn't drink in Rattigan's. They had no children, so we didn't hear about them on the stickball courts.

They were, in fact, the first real people I ever heard described as mysterious. In the summer my brother Tommy and I would go up to the roof, which served as our yard, and sometimes we would lie at the very edge and stare down into their yard. The Orient, to us, was where Terry Lee and Pat Ryan met the Dragon Lady. It was the land of Fu Manchu. It was where Lamont Cranston had gained the power to cloud men's minds. And so we would lie there, our heads full of Macao and Shanghai, listening to the hum of the summer insects, imagining underground tunnels and hidden rooms, incense burning in bowls, terrible poisons, awful tortures. But we never saw the Chinese men.

One Friday night when I was twelve, a sudden summer storm smashed into Brooklyn. Trees went over in Prospect Park. The sewers flooded. A cornice blew off a rooftop on the corner of Fifteenth Street and crushed a parked car. And our clothesline went down, right into the yard of the Chinese men.

When the rain stopped, I was told to go down to the yard and gather the fallen clothes. I didn't want to go. I certainly didn't want to go alone into that mysterious jungle, and my kid brother would be away most of the day, serving as an altar boy at the Saturday weddings. On the other hand, we could not afford to lose any clothes. So down I went to the street.

I walked around to Eleventh Street and faced the house. The blackout shades were drawn on all the windows of the two-story house. I knew it should be an easy thing to do: ring the bell, ask permission to go into the yard, retrieve the clothes and come home. But I was afraid of that house. Afraid to walk through those mysterious rooms, with their secret panels, their smell of incense, their hidden tunnels and dark secrets.

So I went around to Twelfth Street and through the cellar of Billy Rossiter's building. His yard was separated from the Chinese men's by a fence. On Billy's side, the space was bald of foliage, the packed earth muddy from the hard night's rain and the fence smooth and sheer. I turned a garbage can over, climbed on top of it, grabbed the fence and pulled myself up.

I found myself staring into another world. It was colder there, darker. Everything was dank and dripping, as water seeped down the trunks of the weed trees to nourish the wild roots; the banana-shaped leaves were glossy with raindrops; the grass was tangled and riotous, the yard itself a dark seething green, spotted by daubs of white and red and blue from the fallen clothes. The smell was sweet and sickly, as if something had died.

I took a deep breath and dropped to the ground. The weeds and bushes made a rustling sound as I fell to the loamy earth. I huddled there for a long moment. When I stood up, the wild grass reached to my waist. I was certain that snakes were moving through the tangle.

I pushed through green leathery leaves, grabbing for clothes and tucking them under my arm. And then looked at the house of the Chinese men. There was a back door, a small mold-covered stoop at its foot and a window on each side. One of the blackout shades was raised about six inches. A yellow light burned inside, like a signal of temptation. And I realized that for the first time I would be able to see the inside of this mysterious house: the house of the Orient, belonging to people with the power to cloud men's minds.

Hugging the wall of the tenement and staying low, I edged over to the window. I had a clear view. The tall Chinese man was sitting in a chair, smoking a cigarette, his back to the window. The shorter one lay on a tattered couch against the far wall, wearing his sweater, staring at the ceiling.

At the stove, her back to both of them, stood a Chinese woman.

She was young, with black hair streaming to her waist, and she was beautiful. I had never seen her before, not in the grocery store, not in the street. She must have arrived in the night and stayed indoors since.

Then the man on the couch sat up straight and stared right at me, his eyes wide with alarm. He said something and the tall one turned, as did the woman, and I started for the fence. I slipped in the tangled weeds, got up, stumbled again and heaved the clothes into Rossiter's yard. I heard the door opening behind me, scraping against the stoop, and a man's voice barking guttural phrases.

I didn't look back. I grabbed a crossbeam, lifted myself, scrambling against the wet wood, clawed for the top, missed, fell, went up again and reached the top. I hauled myself up and over into the mud and clothes on the other side. I sat there, my heart thumping in my chest, and then gathered the clothing and ran to the cellar and out to the street.

They left that night. Nobody saw them go. But on Sunday morning a crowd of kids gathered in the front yard, peering through the raised shades into the empty rooms. Someone said the Chinese must have been afraid of the immigration people. They were probably ship jumpers, one of the men said. You know, illegals.

A few weeks later, new people moved in. They hacked away the jungle. The cats vanished. We saw bicycles in the yard now and a plastic wading pool and a man who listened to Dodger games on the radio. We didn't look down there much anymore. But sometimes on hot summer evenings, once all the lights were out, I would get up and go to the kitchen window, hoping for the jungle, the drawn shades, the yellow eyes of cats moving in the grass, along with all the other things that were in the yard before I had robbed myself of its mystery. But all I ever saw were the bikes and the moonlight shimmering on the still water of the wading pool. On those nights I would sometimes dream of a beautiful Chinese woman walking through half-lit rooms. Once she even smiled.

M

ULLIGAN loved women. He loved tall women and short women. He loved blondes, brunettes and redheads. Most of the time, he liked them as thin and bony as sparrows, but for three months he went out with a jolly fat girl he called Tons of Fun. There was no end to the mystery of women, their sweetness and infinite variety.

Women were his true vocation. During the day he worked at a dull, slogging job in one of the city agencies. He moved paper, stamped it, shuffled it from one wire basket to another. He sent out form letters he knew would never be read. He typed reports destined to gather dust until they were fed to a shredder.

But women kept him going. Through the long, sour days in the gray building on Chambers Street, Mulligan imagined the details of intricate affairs. He planned strategies and tactics. On yellow pads he listed places where the lights were muted and the music romantic. He knew every menu in Manhattan and every motel in New Jersey. In his mind he danced like Fred Astaire and uttered his lines like Richard Burton. He cruised with women on imaginary yachts and flew great distances on imaginary airplanes.

Every day after work, he went straight to the gym. He always put himself through a hard workout, keeping himself narrow in the waist and muscled across the chest. He had his hair trimmed every week, in places that charged more than he had once paid for a suit. He was always on time for his dates. And on nights when he had no date, he cruised the singles bars. Mulligan spent additional money every few months to learn the new dances, but for him it was worth it.

"If it wasn't for women," he once said, "I'd go into a monastery."

His apartment was the reverse of a monk's cell. The kitchen refrigerator was usually bare, except for ice and limes and chilled vodka. But the bar was always stocked. He had modeled his hi-fi setup on a *Playboy* spread and had taken four years to find an apartment with a working fireplace. The rug was a deep shag, the music always soft and the lighting even dimmer than in the restaurants.

When he hit thirty-five, Mulligan had a small crisis. Age was catching up. He was, it occurred to him, half of seventy. He looked more carefully at his hair in the mirror. He did exercises to keep the jowls tight. He put in an extra half-hour each evening in the gym. All his friends were married and some of their kids were about to graduate from high school. When reminded of these things, Mulligan smiled that cocky smile he had practiced so often in the bathroom mirror.

"I'm the last free guy from the old crowd," he said, "and they all hate me for it. Especially the wives."

When he hit forty, Mulligan didn't smile as much but didn't really change. The hair was a little thinner and there were lines in his face, but he liked to think of himself as looking like "middle William Holden." He still met a lot of women, except that now most of them were older or divorced.

One night last spring he went to Maxwell's Plum and asked a girl to join him for a drink. She smiled sadly. "Come on, mister. You're old enough to be my father."

Mulligan looked at her as if she were insane and went to the movies alone. He saw *A Bridge Too Far* and thought he saw lines beginning to creep into Robert Redford's face. He felt a little better. If it could happen to Redford, it could happen to anyone. And it wasn't hurting Redford, was it?

A few days later, Mulligan had a date with a thirty-four-year-old waitress from Forest Hills. She had glossy black hair and a nice smile. She was also divorced, with three children. That same day at lunch, Mulligan had met a twenty-eight-year-old typist from the Bronx, whom he was going to see the next night, but he wanted to bring the waitress up to what he still described as his pad. She was big, experienced, nice. She told him to meet her on the steps of the New York Public Library, on Forty-second Street and Fifth Avenue, and Mulligan skipped the gym in order to make it there at six o'clock. He looked spectacular: his suit sharply pressed, his teeth gleaming, his hair brushed forward (a trick he had picked up from TV anchormen who needed to hide receding hairlines).

The waitress never showed. Mulligan waited for an hour. He tried to remember whether she'd said the Forty-second Street steps or the Fifth Avenue steps. He moved back and forth between the entrances, pacing angrily. He ran his hands through his hair, fingering it as if it were something precious. Then he went into the library.

He hadn't been in a library for twenty-five years, and that was for some report back in high school. If Mulligan needed a book, he bought it. His last purchase was Kenneth Clark's *Civilization,* which looked good on the coffee table next to his couch. He had seen two episodes on TV and that was enough for him to use the book as a prop for small talk.

The library was crowded, mostly with young people, all of them carrying around stacks of books. Mulligan wandered around for a while, not thinking about much except the missing waitress. Then, as he walked the massive marble halls and staircases looking into this room and that, he began to think about the books that the people around him were so busily perusing. Novels, histories, essays, books on art and music, psychology and child care. There seemed no end to their number, their mystery, their sweetness, their infinite variety.

"I looked at all those books and I wanted to die," Mulligan told me later. "All I could think about was women. I could never get to the end of them. I could never read all the books if I started there and went for the rest of my life. I could never get all the women, either."

The next night Mulligan met the typist for dinner. She was nice. He was polite. He drove her home to the Bronx. A month later they were married. It was a very nice ceremony. They had the reception in the Chateau Pelham in the Bronx. They went to Bermuda for the honeymoon. The last time I saw him, he was moving to the Island. His pants were looking baggy. He was carrying a copy of *Trinity* and was combing his hair back off his brow.

ALL through his eleventh summer, Coffey worshiped Billy Boy Devine. He would sit on the stoop of the front yard on Garfield Place until Billy Boy came home, waiting for the game to begin. There was always a game, even when it rained, and Billy Boy Devine was the best stickball player Coffey had ever seen. That was the thing Coffey always remembered; that and the fact that Billy Boy's wife had red hair. And the way Billy Boy left Garfield Place forever.

But all that, the bad part, happened in August. In June Billy Boy would rush home from the riggers' shop at the Navy Yard— his nails black, his undershirt pasted to his back—and wave to his wife, who sat quietly at the window. The big guys in the saloon would come out, laughing and punching one another, and someone would bring the cardboard container of beer, someone else would open a hydrant to wash the court and then they would play.

Billy Boy lived on the first floor right and Coffey lived with his brothers and mother on the top floor left, and when school ended for the summer, Billy Boy made Coffey the official scorer for the big guys.

"Just get the numbers right, kid," Billy Boy told him. "Nothin' else really matters."

The game was all that really mattered and Coffey loved the ferocity of Billy Boy's style: the way he slashed at the ball, the way he ran the bases, his legs a blur, his eyes burning, snorting as he turned second base, staring out past the bases at the outfield. He was the first great athlete Coffey had ever known.

But the boy never saw the red-headed wife very clearly. He often passed her in the hall as she clutched the grocery bags from the A & P, and he once bumped into her at the mailboxes. But he felt something strange and overwhelming when he was near her.

He would swallow and move on, without looking, as if looking at her would somehow be a betrayal of Billy Boy.

Later Coffey couldn't remember exactly when it had started with the hoodlum. He remembered seeing the guy around, his hair slicked back, wearing maroon Ali Baba pants with pistol pockets and a three-inch rise. He never played ball. Hoodlums never did. Instead, when the others started playing, he would watch a few minutes, looking at Billy Boy, and then move off along the avenue. Once the boy saw him eating alone in the Purity Diner on Union Street. Another time he saw him driving down the avenue in a maroon Buick, playing the radio loud and flexing the muscles in his left arm as he moved the wheel. He never heard him talk.

One steaming midnight in July, Coffey woke up, breathless from the heat, and went out to sleep on the fire escape. And he saw the maroon Buick halfway down the block, parked on the dark side of the street. He watched it for a while and then saw Billy Boy's wife step out and walk quickly up the block in the shadows, smoothing her red hair. Coffey wanted to die.

For the next few weeks, Coffey kept score during the games and the rest of the time watched the red-haired wife of Billy Boy Devine. She would go out in the mornings, after Billy Boy went to the Navy yard, and sometimes late at night, after Billy Boy went to sleep. Coffey felt that he, too, was part of a plot against the great ballplayer and several times tried to tell him, but the words just wouldn't come.

After a while, he wasn't alone. He heard the women talk, saw the smirks when Billy Boy came home, and soon the man in the maroon Buick started coming around openly, pulling up in front of the house to wait for the red-haired woman. He was a hoodlum and had to act like a hoodlum. On Garfield Place they started talking about the way the horns had fallen upon Billy Boy Devine. And everyone waited to see what he would do.

One August afternoon Coffey came home early from Coney Island, sunburned and gritty with sand. There were three squad cars and an ambulance from the Methodist Hospital in front of the house. Across the street a crowd of women from the block stared at the house, nodding and murmuring; the guys from the bar were out on the corner. The block was silent.

Coffey started up the stoop and a cop stopped him. "Outside, kid," the cop said. Coffey said that he lived there, on the top floor, his name was Coffey, look at the bells. The cop looked at the bells and let the boy through. "Go straight up, kid," the cop said sadly. "No hangin' around." There were more cops in front of Billy Boy's apartment, some of them in plain clothes. As Coffey started up the stairs, he looked past the cops into the kitchen and saw Billy Boy.

He was sitting on a chair, his eyes open very wide, staring straight ahead. Behind him was his red-haired wife, half on the bed, half off. She was wearing a green dress, and one leg jutted out like a broken white tube. Her throat had been cut. The bed was soaked with blood.

Coffey ran upstairs. Nobody was home, and he went to the front and crawled out on the fire escape and watched the squad cars and the old women and guys from the bar. He looked for the Buick but the hoodlum must have heard what happened. After a while the cops took Billy Boy out, looking limp and drained. They had his hands cuffed behind his back and they put him in a squad car and drove off. Coffey sat on the fire escape, tears rolling down his face, knowing that he would never keep score for Billy Boy Devine again. He had a beautiful wife and her hair was red, but not as red as blood.

L A T E Saturday night in the frozen city, at the bar of Johnny's Lounge on Eighth Avenue, Irizarry the Mechanic was telling a story. A half-dozen of the hard-core regulars were hanging around, and the waitresses shivered every time the door opened.

"This Puerto Rican was driving a hundred penguins to the zoo," Irizarry said. "They're all in the back, dig, all squash together. He's drivin' up the Jersey Turnpike when he gets four flats. He gets out, an' he is tired, man, an' he is disgusted, an' he knows he had to get these penguins to the zoo, dig? But he got these four flat tires."

"Where he get the penguins, man?" said Cuban Phillie.

"Shuddup, don't interrupt. Anyway, he looks over on the grass and sees this Polack standin' under a tree."

"Hey, no Polish jokes in here," said Johnny the Owner. "We got any Polish customers here, they get mad."

"I never seen no Polish customers here," said Cuban Phillie. "What Polish customers?"

"Stanley," said Johnny. "The guy comes in days."

"Okay, he sees this *Cuban* standin' under a tree," Irizarry said, "an' he says, 'Hey, you, come over here!' So the Cuban comes over. 'Hey, you wanna hundred dollars?' the P.R. says to the Cuban. An' the Cuban says 'Sure.' So the P.R. goes aroun' the back of the truck and opens the door an' he says, 'Take these penguins to the zoo.' "

"I like this story better with a Pole in it," said Cuban Phillie.

"The Cuban looks at the penguins and he says okay. They take down a ramp and these penguins all walk out. A hundred of them, see, all black and white, and they waddle around with their arms at their sides, and the Cuban gets at the front and takes the hundred dollars, and they start off for New York."

"Can't you make the guy Jewish?"

"The Puerto Rican sees this Howard Johnson's and he checks in and goes to sleep," Irizarry went on. "Three hours later he wakes up and he calls a car service."

"Hey, wait a minute. They don't got a car service in Jersey. They only got car service in Brooklyn and the Bronx," said Cuban Phillie.

"Lemme tell the story," said Irizarry. "So the P.R. gets in the car to go to New York. He just leaves the truck there and heads right for New York. He's zoomin' along, through the toll booth, down into the Lincoln Tunnel and up the other side, and they're in New York. The cab pulls around and starts across Forty-second Street. He hits Eighth Avenue. And then, on the other side of the street, he sees the Cuban walkin' along with the hundred penguins—in the wrong direction!"

"Heading back to Jersey," Johnny says, laughing.

"Exactly," Irizarry said. "So he says to the cabdriver, 'Stop the car.' The guy stops and the P.R. gets out and yells at the Cuban, 'Hey, you, I thought I told you to take those penguins to the zoo!' The Cuban stops and looks at him an' says, 'I did. But I got some money left and so *now I'm takin' them to the movies*!' "

They all laughed except Cuban Phillie, who ordered a double Bacardi on the rocks. Black Henry, who had been very quiet, cleared his throat.

"This brother had a real high IQ," he said. "An' this gave him real bad trouble. In Harlem the other brothers thought he was snob. He couldn't get down with them. He couldn't say 'dig' an' 'wow' and he couldn't call his woman 'man.' But downtown he had trouble too. The white folks thought he was uppity. They thought he was so smart, he just was bound to give them trouble. An' all because he had this two-sixty IQ."

"You sure he wasn't Cuban, man?" said Cuban Phillie.

Black Henry kept talking: "So he reads about this cat has a machine can shave points off your IQ. An' he goes down to see this doctor and tells him his problem. The guy says sure, he can shave off, oh, maybe thirty points. The machine shaves off two points a minute. The brother says, 'Let's do it,' and the doctor straps him in the chair. He puts the electrodes on his head, he straps his hands down, he makes him look like Frankenstein, and he turns on the switch and tells the guy he'll be back in fifteen minutes."

Black Henry sipped his beer. Irizarry was already laughing.

"This doctor had a quick dentist appointment right across the street, so he rushes over and goes up to the dentist and gets his X-ray and shoots the breeze with the dentist, and then he goes out to the elevator and gets in. Well, the elevator gets stuck with this doctor in it. They on like the fifty-ninth floor, man, and the brother is across the street, still strapped in the chair, man, losin' two points a minute.

"It takes them an hour and a half to fix the elevator, and the doctor runs out, right through traffic, into the street, with everybody honkin' their horns and a cop blowin' a whistle, and' he runs into his building and takes the elevator upstairs. He gets his key out, opens the door, runs down the hall into the room, pulls off the electrodes, unstraps the brother's arm, shuts off the juice and says to him, 'Hey, how do you feel?'

"The brother get up, straightens his tie an' says, *'Muy bien,* man. *Muy bien.'* "

Johnny the Owner fell against the wall, laughing. Irizarry started hitting Black Henry with a *Daily News.*

"I don't get it," said Cuban Phillie.

They all laughed again and this time Irizarry hit Cuban Phillie with the *Daily News.* The door opened and Blonde Carmen came in. Everybody shivered.

"Hey," she said, "you hear about the Irishman who ran into a crowded firehouse and yelled 'Movie, movie!' "?

"Everybody's a comedian tonight," said Johnny.

"What do the numbers 1492 and 1776 have in common?" Blonde Carmen asked me.

"I dunno."

"They're adjoining rooms in the Dublin Hilton."

I borrowed Irizarry's paper and gave her a whack.

"These two Puerto Rican astronauts are out in space," said Black Henry. "The one dude has to go out for a space walk. He is on a cable and he closes the door behind him. The other P.R. is lying around reading *El Diario.* Suddenly there's a knock at the door. The dude looks up and says, *'Who is it?'* "

"If you think that's funny," said Blonde Carmen, "then you oughta get the hell out of here."

"This guy's walkin' along a street in Ponce," Irizarry said, "and suddenly he hears a mysterious voice that says, 'Roulette. San Juan. Roulette. San Juan.' He goes home that night and he sits on the porch while his wife cooks and he hears the voice again: 'Roulette. San Juan.' He goes in and tells his wife and says it's an omen. She says, 'Hey, I know what you want. You want to go to San Juan with some chick and play roulette. Don't make up no stories.'

"So that night he's lying in bed and he hears the voice again: 'Roulette. San Juan. Roulette. San Juan.' He wakes up his wife, tells her to be quiet and listen. An' she hears the voice too: 'Roulette. San Juan. Roulette. San Juan.' He figures it's an omen for sure and so does she.

"The next day they go to the bank. He has seventeen thousand dollars in the bank, the money they saved for ten years, and he tells the guy to give him three thousand dollars. But he hears the voice again. 'Take it all,' says the voice. 'Take it all.' So he takes out the whole seventeen thousand and him and his wife go to San Juan to play roulette.

"They go to a casino and he hears the voice: 'Thirty-three. Play thirty-three.' So he puts a thousand down on thirty-three. Then he hears the voice again: 'No, bet it all. Bet it all.' The guy running the roulette wheel has to ask the manager to let the guy bet the seventeen thousand. The manager gives the okay, and the guy from Ponce bets the whole works, his whole life savings, on thirty-three. The wheel spins, he's nervous as hell, he figures any minute he'll be rich. The wheel slows down. And it stops on twelve. He stands there wiped out. His wife is crying. And the voice says, 'Well . . . we blew that one.' "

"That's it," Johnny said. "I'm closing."

"This Irishman, this Jew and this Puerto Rican were crossing the desert," Blonde Carmen began. "The Irishman had a bottle of beer, the Jew had a pastrami sandwich and the Puerto Rican was carrying a car door—"

"Basta," Johnny said. "Last call."

C O N D O N had not seen his daughter for almost a year, and when she walked in the door of Elaine's, it took him a few long moments to recognize her. Her hair was long now, in the straight, flat style of California blondes, and she was thinner and seemed taller. A few loners at the bar turned to look at her, and she moved through the early evening crowd with the ease of someone used to being looked at. The baby fat is gone, Condon thought, melted away. I'm old.

"Hello, Daddy," she said, squeezing his hand and brushing his cheek with a cool kiss. "You look fine."

"You too, sweetheart." He moved a chair to let her sit beside him against the wall. I'm a liar, Condon thought. She doesn't look fine. Those eyes don't look fine at all. He waved Nick over, and she ordered a stinger and talked a little about San Francisco, how scary it was, and he asked her what she thought of Patricia Hearst.

"I think she was right," his daughter said. "She had to have more fun sticking up banks than living with that family."

"Uh-oh," Condon said.

"Oh, Daddy, come on," she said. "I'm not talking about you. I'm talking about them. Her family."

"Well, I hope so," he said, smiling, thinking that now, at nineteen, she had her mother's high cheekbones, the skin pulled taut across them. Her eyes moved around the room like hers did, too. The waiter brought drinks. She ordered veal, he asked for a steak.

A party of people in dinner jackets and long gowns, heavy with cologne and chatter, moved dreamily past them. Several of the men had powdery faces and wore silver makeup on their eyelids. A fortyish blond woman with violet lips and impossibly

lush breasts drifted past the cigarette machine, crossing paths with Rudolf Nureyev as she moved. A press agent stopped at Condon's table.

"It's that Frankenstein movie," he explained. "You know, one of those Andy Warhol jobs." The blonde drifted by again. "That's Monique Van Vooren. She's in the thing."

Condon shrugged. He did not understand the world anymore. His daughter smiled but there was still something wrong with her eyes. They talked about music and movies, and the food arrived.

"What is it, kiddo?" Condon asked.

"I don't know what you mean."

"Something's on your mind, isn't it?"

She waved her hand slightly, dismissing the discussion, and poked a knife at her veal. The place was packed now with the Warhol crowd and Condon exchanged glances with Elaine; she shrugged a saloon keeper's shrug that said, Well, it's that kind of night. Condon felt the contact slipping away, as if it were too late to ever talk again to his daughter, and he was sorry for that. He wanted to tell her how lonely he had become, how these days he would walk around town like some ruined old man, dreamy with the past.

"Did you ever hear of Augie Galan?" he asked her suddenly. No, she hadn't. Her face was blank, then puzzled, and Condon told her that he was just a ballplayer who, in the old days, played for Brooklyn. I'd like to tell you about him, Condon thought, and about Kirby Higbe and Whitlow Wyatt and Pete Reiser; tell you about the day the *Normandie* burned and we all went over to see it; or the way we came home in the evenings to listen to the *Inner Sanctum,* the *Kraft Music Hall* and Stan Lomax with today's doings in the world of sports. He watched the Warhol crowd move around and felt sloppy and fat, rheumy with cheap nostalgia, crowded with mistakes and failure. Christ, he thought, I'd like to get married again.

"Yes, there is something, Dad," she said quietly, laying down the knife and fork and setting her hands on the lip of the table. There was a look in her eyes that he had not seen since the day, ten years before, when he had taken her to the boarding school. Wary, expecting the worst.

"I had an abortion," she said. "Three weeks ago."

He touched both of her hands. "Sweetheart."

"Oh, it was okay, Dad." Her voice was frail in the noisy restaurant. "I mean, it's a simple thing now. It really was, Dad."

"Why didn't you call—"

"It was my problem, Dad," she said. "I wanted to handle it myself." She took one of his cigarettes and he lit it for her. "And I did, all by myself."

He remembered a day at the beach when the August thunder had split the night and he had hugged her and told her that everything would be all right. She was so small then, he thought, that she fit in my arms.

"I wish you had called me," he said. "I could have helped."

Condon called for the check, paid it and then walked with her through the crowd out to Second Avenue.

"Are you angry with me?" she asked.

"No. You're my daughter. I love you."

"Thank you." She took his arm as they walked down Second Avenue to pick up the papers and go home. Maybe if I tried harder, Condon thought, I could explain about Augie Galan.

FOR weeks Gelhorn could not sleep. He tossed and moved in the big bed on the second floor, listening to the sounds of Queens at night. Fragments of faces, remembered conversations and scraps of music moved through his consciousness like memories of an artillery barrage: real but disordered. In the morning the bed was damp, the sheets twisted and sometimes torn. After a while his wife moved into the room where the boys had slept before they grew up and moved away.

On this Sunday, while his wife slept, he made the coffee alone, watching the day break gray and wintry in the yard. The ravaged lawn was mottled with dirty snow, the apple tree dead for the season. He looked at the paper but did not read it, as pieces of the night pushed their way forward.

He thought of Perkins, with the hard flat face and the laconic Southern accent, chewing tobacco the way New Yorkers chewed Dentyne, laughing over the Sad Sack and Private Breger and Willie and Joe. Perkins, who wanted to sleep for a week with Rita Hayworth, and who used to take the pinups out of *Yank* and erase the lines where the bathing suits ended.

Perkins was standing beside Sergeant Gavin, with his yellow California hair, finicky manners, soapy blue eyes. And the third one, heavy, with skin that flushed in the cold when they finally got to the forest in Belgium and hard eyes that lay in his soft face like stones in custard.

"What the hell was his name?" Gelhorn said out loud, his voice startling him; he hoped his wife was still asleep.

Harrigan. Marty Harrigan.

He sipped the black coffee and tried to erase the faces of the dead. He went to the hall closet and put on a coat.

There were a few children playing in the yards, but the avenue was deserted. He walked to the subway, catching a reflection of himself in store windows: a lumpy man now, the coat covering his swollen bulk, his face finally old.

And he remembered Perkins that time in London, when the tall, stringy English paratrooper said that the trouble with the Yanks was that they were oversexed, overpaid, and over here. Gelhorn told him to shut up, and the paratrooper called Gelhorn a kike, and Perkins stepped in and dropped the right hand on the paratrooper's jaw. They had to fight everybody in the place, tables going over and women screaming and hands reaching out.

Jesus, that was the best time, Gelhorn thought as he went down the steps into the subway, heading for the city. And what the hell happened? Perkins was supposed to be a bigot, a Southerner, but there he was, fighting the whole British Empire because someone called his friend a kike. Shoulder to shoulder. Backs to the bar. Throwing punches. And later they told Gavin and Harrigan, and they got sore too and wanted to come back into London and wipe out anybody who was left. And then the laughing and singing . . . *There'll be bluebirds over the white cliffs of Dover, tomorrow, when the world is free* . . .

We believed it all, Gelhorn thought: killing Nazis, stopping Hitler, destroying Germany, all of it straight, clean and uncomplicated. Out on a summer drill field, we would shiver when they raised the flag and played "The Star-Spangled Banner."

The train roared under the river, its walls painted with the names of strangers. Just once more, he wished, I would like to see "Kilroy was here" written in a public place. But Kilroy is dead, and so are Perkins and Gavin and Harrigan and that crazy nurse . . . Mansfield. Helen Mansfield. Her crooked smile and the dimpled chin.

He was smiling when he came up into Times Square. The old song moved through his head . . . *Joy and laughter and peace ever after, tomorrow, just you wait and see.* I want to see a movie, Gelhorn thought. He stood beside the statue of Father Duffy, but the cold marquees offered only cop pictures and skin flicks.

He walked up to the park and looked at the ruined earth and the choked dead lake at Fifty-ninth Street and thought about the ruined forests in the Ardennes, the Germans coming in a lumpy tide through the fog, and how all of them had died that winter of the Bulge, even those who walked out of it.

After a while he walked back to the subway. Maybe tonight I'll sleep, he thought . . . And remembered Perkins throwing the right hand and wondered which European cross he was buried under. It felt like snow.

M A L L O Y awoke from a dreamless sleep and reached for the cigarettes. A gray morning light struggled through the drapes, and he heard the first sharp details of the day's long noise: the backfire of a bus, a door slamming on a bread truck, the churning sound of a Sanitation Department sweeper. Later they would melt with a thousand other sounds into one long drilling New York noise, but now, in the morning, he played at identifying them, imagining the faces of the drivers, the passengers, the winos on the corner. And all the while he knew that it was still only four or five o'clock on the Coast, that it would be hours yet before he got the call and that perhaps he would not get it at all.

He smashed the cigarette out and tried to return to sleep. But the sounds of the street were rising the six stories to his room and sleep would not come. He suddenly remembered his son's wounded face on the day he brought him to the school in Vermont, and he lit another cigarette and got out of bed, as if movement could drive that day from his memory.

He smoked and shaved: a drag, a stroke, carving through the white lather, wishing there were some new way to perform the ritual, conscious of the rust stains on the sink, and he remembered the great bathroom they had the first year in California after the third novel hit and everyone wanted him to write for the movies. There were two sinks and two showers and a dressing room for his wife and a view over the valley, and for a while he thought it would go on forever. It was 1971 now, not 1964, and most of Hollywood was gone and so was most of everything else he had that year.

He finished shaving, dropped a scalding washcloth on his face and walked across the room, still calculating the time on the

Coast, and threw open the drapes. A heavyset Puerto Rican man was sweeping the sidewalk in front of the Y, while a pretty girl with net stockings waited at the bus stop with her hair in curlers, watching the traffic coagulate at the corner of Seventh Avenue. When you could see what made it, he thought, the noise was not so persistent. He turned to the desk.

All of what he had become was there: a meager short story typed painfully on yellow second sheets, a clipping from *Newsweek* about a man who tracked down the killer of his son, three old treatments bound in dog-eared black covers from Studio Duplicating, the discarded beginning of a movie about a soldier of fortune, the cop story that he finished three weeks before *The French Connection* opened, a book about a female spy that someone wanted him to make into a movie, if he would write it on spec. And the bills from the hotel and the stores, the last jagged letter from his son, the notice from the accountant that he was now two months behind in his alimony, the note from his agent saying that the British were not interested in a collection of his short stories. He had fallen into hack work; it was what he did instead of writing, and writing was what he did instead of living.

He remembered how it used to come roaring out of him: novels and short stories and movies. He had more energy than five men then, and now he was waiting for a phone call. If he could leave, he would rent a car and drive up to the school and see his son. But he could not leave; he could not go out, and now, eight months off the sauce, even the old solace of saloons was beyond him. He typed "Fade In" again, stopped and then stood up. He picked *Wind, Sand and Stars* from the bookshelf, lay down on the bed and for a while became an airline pilot in the days when flying was still romantic, crossing the vast emptiness of the Sahara, and after a while he slept.

The phone woke him at noon. The agent had heard from Universal. They were sorry but it just didn't seem right for them. They liked it, all right, but not for them. Keep in touch, they said, maybe we can find something we agree on. And that was that. He sat for a long time on the bed and then called his ex-wife.

"I'm going up to see Bobby," he said.

"Please don't."

"I have to."

"You'll just upset him, Robert. Please don't."

"I want to talk to him," Malloy said.

"He doesn't want to talk to you."

"Who the hell does?" he said.

"What?"

"I said, 'Who the hell does?' Who wants to talk to me? You don't want to talk to me. My own son doesn't want to talk to me. I'd just like to talk to someone."

"Are you all right, Robert?" she asked.

"I'm just great."

"Are you writing?"

"Checks."

"Christ, self-pity is boring."

"Go to hell."

He hung up, dressed quickly and went out into the day. A hard wind was blowing off the river, scrubbing the air. He headed downtown, hugging the sides of the buildings, drifting toward the Lion's Head. He would not be going to Vermont. I should go up there and see him and take him out of that place and just leave. Drive to the West. Or find our way to Florida. Show him the training camps and swim in the Gulf. Let his body brown in the sun. I could get work in a bar or at some small-town newspaper. Births and deaths and fires. I wrote that stuff once; I can write it again.

He passed the flower markets in the Twenties. Young Latin men stomped their feet to keep warm or worked at the displays, placing the brightest colored flowers in front. I need color: green foliage, the orange sea of Bonnard, the azure sky. The headline of the *Post* screamed from a newsstand: RUBOUT! A gangster with the front of his face blown off. Births and deaths and fires. I could change my name and write all of that again. It would be better than living in a cheap room in the Thirty-fourth Street YMCA. It would be better than waiting for a call from a movie producer who can't read.

At Sheridan Square he stood on the corner watching the wind toss dust and paper across the avenue. And then he went into the Lion's Head. It was dark and almost empty. Tommy, the bartender, came over.

"What'll it be, Robert?"

"Whiskey," Malloy said.

He looked out through the barred windows and the words "Fade In" slowly typed themselves into his brain, and he began to describe the high winds over the Sahara and the Bedouin tribes below and the clustered French soldiers in the wadi, and he remembered the thin trail of smoke rising from Fort Zinderneuf.

"Water on the side," he said.

"Sure thing," Tommy said.

ON the last day, Donovan lay alone in the beach house, listening to the sea. The bed sheet was gritty with sand and he had a thick brown taste in his mouth from the savage night before, but Donovan didn't move. He listened carefully, trying to imagine how far the waves broke and ran on the beach. He picked out the sounds of three slamming car doors, and he heard the cars move along the gravel road and then the sound of his children coming closer to the house, the boy's reedy voice, the girl's thin, persistent plea. He lay quietly, his eyes closed, and then heard his wife in the kitchen, the screen door slapping shut behind her and talk that was more a texture than actual voices, and then the door slamming again and the empty roar of the sea.

In the morning of the next day, somehow he would go to the studio and try to do what he always did on the first day after a vacation. He couldn't surrender routine now: he would get black coffee and a cheese Danish at the Central Luncheonette, the bottom of the bag wet in his hand from the leaking container, and go up to the studio, unlock the door with the free hand, put the coffee on the drawing table and switch on all the lights. And drinking the coffee, inhaling the first cigarette of the day, he would start. He did mechanicals and paste-ups for advertising agencies and he was very good at it; he was fast, very clean and accurate, and it had been a long time since he had thought about being a painter. But he thought briefly about it now, lying alone in the sandy bed, thought about the thick impasto textures he could build on canvas or the streaked effect of casein on wax, before he reached for the cigarettes, took a long drag on a Camel and drove the old dream out of his head.

After a while his wife came back in and opened the door to the bedroom.

"We're going," she said.

He didn't say anything; the sea made a sloshing sound.

"I said we're going."

"I'll call you during the week," Donovan said.

"That's all? Don't you want to say goodbye to them?"

"No."

She turned abruptly and went out, and he tried to remember the first time he had seen her. The moment would not come; he knew the year, remembered some of the songs and the general undefinable mood, but he could not recall the specific moment. In some ways it didn't matter and in other ways it mattered very much. He took a drag and held it a long time, not wanting to hear the sounds of departure.

Instead, his head filled with her face the night before, twisted with resentment and something that was probably hatred. It had built all day, from that lunch with the kids on the beach. There had been a black girl in a bikini. Donovan stared at her, drawing her in his mind, the charcoal defining her sacral triangle above and between the buttocks, and then curving radically to capture the incredible buttocks themselves. She was very black, almost blue, with an orange bikini. She had small breasts, but he thought that her ass looked like a bowling ball split in two, the halves laid side by side. She moved with absolute knowledge of the way she looked. A dancer, he thought. Or a jock.

"You're a disgusting fool," his wife said quietly. He tried again to explain that he looked at women's bodies with a cold eye. He had been trained as an artist. He looked at bodies aesthetically, he said, enjoying their proportions, their planes and volumes. And, hey, he insisted, I never do anything. I just look. They're like pictures in a gallery. I can love Rembrandt without wanting to sleep with him. I was an artist. Remember?

"Some artist," she snorted, took the children by their hands and walked off down the beach. Donovan did not protest. He did not follow. He drank most of a thermos of vodka and tonic, thinking that he had had enough of her. He had changed his life for her. He had accepted stupid work and surrendered old dreams. Just to feed her. To make a home. To pay for children. To afford these summers in the Hamptons. And I look at a woman's body, he thought, and she snarls at me. He got up when the wind turned cold. His wife had not returned. He gathered the blanket and the various sandals and the empty thermos and walked back through the dunes to the cottage. There was no sign of the black girl. She was like so many others he had seen on subways and street corners, in the lobbies of theaters, in department stores and coffee shops. She had appeared, been consumed with his eyes and had gone.

Two other couples were coming for dinner and Donovan was cooking a giant beef stew. In the kitchen he chopped the beef, potatoes, celery, carrots. He peeled the onions. He drank more vodka. His wife returned in chilly silence but the noisy clatter of the children eased his anger. He busied himself in the kitchen. The two couples arrived. The wives joined his wife on the porch. The men drank and talked about the Yankees and drank and laughed at familiar jokes and drank. Donovan laughed louder than the others, moving from table to stove, adding spices, improvising, thinking of Picasso's wild energy with paint, or Schwitters making a collage of everything in sight. For hours he built his masterpiece. A stew was like a painting or a collage. Everything could be used. The children ate boiled hot dogs and went to bed. The men drank some more. And then all of them were at the table and Donovan was ladling the stew into stoneware bowls and they started to eat. Silence. One of the women chewed too long. And then his wife rose, carried her bowl to the screen door, opened the door and flung stew and bowl into the sandy yard.

"You cook like you fuck," she said to Donovan, and walked past him out of the kitchen and back to the porch. Right out of his life.

Now he heard the car doors shut heavily, the children's protesting voices thin over the sound of the sea. The car whined into gear, threw up gravel, and they were gone. Donovan released the cigarette smoke, watching it become a thin curl of pale blue against the rose-colored walls of the beach house. He wondered what she was thinking. He pictured her on the Montauk Highway, her thin hands gripping the wheel in dry fury, the children sitting in the back. He remembered the time they drove to the West, through deserts where sun-blasted iceboxes stood beside empty gas stations. He had tried on that trip to make her understand him. They had no kids then but she ignored him, her eyes on the emptiness. He thought, At least understand me. I give you me. Take me and then you can offer me yourself. I want to sleep with you, not just your body. She glanced at him while he talked, but shifted to a discussion of politics, which was her way of saying nothing. She said nothing all the way to California.

Slowly, Donovan got up. He shaved in the thick heat, wondering what he had done on the previous Labor Day and what he would do on the next. He lit another cigarette. He found a last bottle of tonic water in the refrigerator and drank it down greedily, rinsing his mouth. He packed all the garbage into a plastic trash bag and stepped outside. Down the block the Graysons were loading their station wagon. Someone waved. He waved back. He put the trash bag beside the mailbox and went back into the cottage. A radio was playing rock 'n' roll. The traffic was building on the road.

He packed his suitcase, locked the windows and the doors and put the key under the mat. The real estate lady would be around to pick it up after all the summer people had gone. Donovan hoped he wouldn't run into her now. He climbed up through the scrub to the road. The town was two miles from the cottage and the sun had burned away the morning haze. It would be a long, hot walk. He could stay with Malloy, he thought. Malloy had a couch and he was divorced. Malloy would understand. He would stay with Malloy and look for an apartment. In the Village. Or down in Soho. A loft, maybe. If he could afford it. He would have to buy a bed, a table, chairs. He would have to duplicate everything he had accumulated with his wife. Toasters, knives, forks, a radio, a phonograph. One of each, please.

At the Carvel he stopped for a rest and sat on the suitcase. His shirt was soaked through. He mopped his face. An MG came speeding along, small and aggressive. The black girl was sitting on the passenger's side, with a yellow scarf tied tightly around her hair. A bearded white man was driving. The car vanished down the road. Donovan stood up and waved goodbye.

T
H E old actress lunched every day at the Plaza. It remained her favorite hotel in New York because it was the one that had most successfully resisted time. She always lunched alone, at the same corner table, masking herself with tinted glasses and a dark scarf drawn tight at the neck. Strangers seldom recognized her and she liked it that way. Her fans always asked her when she was going to work in a movie again, and she had come to understand that she would probably never work again, ever. There were still a few parts for her to play, but they were ugly remakes of *What Ever Happened to Baby Jane,* scripts with Bette Davis' fingerprints all over them. All horror shows. To make such films, she would have to do violence to her youth.

On this afternoon she took one script to lunch with her, but stopped reading it on page 27, when her character reached for an ax. She waved the waiter over and ordered eggs Benedict and white wine. She watched the young people move through the muted lights of the lobby restaurant, and heard a piano playing somewhere and remembered how it felt the first time she understood that she could not hold back age. The flesh finally curdled: it folded, grew serrated and, without powder and paint, looked like the neck of a turtle.

She hated that moment and the knowledge that she had reached the point where face-lifts and beauty treatments could do nothing. But she remembered thinking that maybe this was part of the scheme of things; perhaps nature ruined the body so death would be more acceptable. She thought more often about death lately and discussed it with the few friends she still had—the old press agent, her last business manager, a few troupers.

The sad thing was that her obituaries would be filled with lies, stitched together from press releases concocted in the golden

years of Hollywood, the years before the war. Her friends often asked her to write a book, just to set the record straight, but she hated books written by old actresses, loaded as they were with false nostalgia and self-pity that bordered on the sinister. Such books were monologues, with the best lines reserved for yourself.

The old movies were the truest record. They still played on the late shows, although not so much anymore on Channel 2, where *The CBS Late Movie* was filled with reruns of *Kojak.* In New York her movies now played on Channel 5 and Channel 9, and in those films she was forever young, her skin clean and pure, her eyes flashing and shimmering in the odd silver aura of black and white. Those handsome leading men were all gone; they were no longer young when she first met them. The sets had been destroyed thirty years ago. Even some of the studios were gone, eaten by time and television. She was glad she would not have to read her obituaries, though for all she knew the newspapers had them prepared and on file.

The waiter brought the eggs and the wine, bowed formally and went away, and when she looked up, a familiar figure stepped hesitantly into the room.

The cowboy hat made him look taller than he really was and his face was glazed from the California sun. But the old director wore a patch over one eye, and she remembered reading that he was having trouble seeing from the other. He was, someone said, almost blind. There was a retrospective at one of the museums, a show of a dozen of his films; she had seen that in one of the magazines. And there he was, beside him a bright young man carrying a tape recorder, and she realized that the director was one of the few people alive who had seen her naked when she was young.

They were making a picture at Warners' that year and she had to run for days through rainy streets on the old back lot to film one critical scene. He was married then and so was she. He called her Buster. We're ready when you are, Buster. Let's run through it again, Buster. And then one evening they were speeding along the Pacific Coast Highway in a yellow roadster, with the sea gargling and moaning on their right as they moved south to Laguna. They ate lobsters in a place on the beach and danced to a Skinnay Ennis record that he played over and over on the jukebox. Finally he said, "Okay, Buster. I guess we'd better stay the night."

She poked at the eggs and sipped the wine. She looked up as the old director moved to a table with the earnest young man. The young man would ask the director about the old days and the director would respond with great stories; she was sure of that. But there were some stories none of them would ever tell.

She sipped the wine, thinking that she should go over to say hello, worrying that he might not be able to see her, wondering if it was true that he couldn't really see out of the good eye. And even if he could see me, she thought, he might not recognize me. I'm not the girl in the yellow roadster anymore.

She poked at the eggs and finished the wine, then called for coffee and the bill. The waiter went away and she glanced over at the director, who was smiling at his companion. The coffee and the bill arrived together and she fumbled through her purse for the cash.

Suddenly the old director was standing at her table.

"Hello, Buster," he said softly.

She started to rise and he touched her on the cheek.

"Still as beautiful as ever," he said, and she pressed her head wordlessly against his chest, wondering whether they could rent a car somewhere and drive out to the sea and eat lobsters and dance a little and maybe even spend the night.

About the Author

Born in Brooklyn in 1935, PETE HAMILL left high school after two years
to become a sheet-metal worker in the Brooklyn Navy Yard. In 1952 he
joined the Navy. Later he studied painting on the GI bill at Pratt Insti-
tute and Mexico City College, worked as a designer and started writing
for newspapers in 1960. Formerly a columnist for the New York *Post* and
the New York *Daily News,* he has also appeared in many other newspapers and magazines. He is the author of five novels—*A Killing for Christ,
The Gift, Flesh and Blood, Dirty Laundry* and *The Deadly Piece*—as well
as a collection of his journalism, *Irrational Ravings.* He has lived in
Mexico, Spain, Italy and Ireland, and now lives again in Brooklyn. He has
two daughters, Adriene and Deirdre.